One Week at the Faraway Inn

A BERKSHIRE ROMANCE

E.A. BRADY

SANDGATE EAST PUBLISHING

Dedication

For Steve. Because they're always for Steve.

If you and I know each other in real life, ***please don't read this book***.
It contains descriptions of sex between two consenting adults.

Should you decide to move forward against my advice, please know
that it may be weird to look each other in the eye the next time we hang
out.

You've been warned.

And I love you for reading it anyway!

Victoria

The further west she drove from Boston, the greener and more spacious the scenery became, and the tighter and more anxious Victoria became. It had been a long time, years in fact, since she had been out of the city for more than a weekend. And never by herself.

As the traffic dwindled to near nothingness in the unending stretch of the Massachusetts Turnpike between Springfield and Stockbridge, Victoria Lathrop's second thoughts about spending a week alone in the Berkshires came crashing back to add to her already high anxiety level. Would she be able to do any of the art classes she'd signed up for or had all her creativity dried up from years of non-use? Did the old adage, *use it or lose it*, apply do artistic abilities?

The logistics of being away from Lathrop Associates, the social media management business in which she'd invested blood, sweat, and tears over the last decade, had all been taken care of. Her clients had been notified of her absence and her co-workers were more than capable of handling whatever came their way. All Victoria had to do was lighten up and enjoy herself over the next seven days. But the question remained: would she be able to do that?

Her schedule had been loosely planned around a mixed media art class, a Boston Symphony Orchestra performance, and a potential mixology class after dinner at an upscale local restaurant. The incredibly vibrant and active art scene coupled with the amazing natural beauty of the area had drawn Victoria to the Berkshires for her mini renaissance. On the eve of her forty-fifth birthday, she had finally taken long-avoided action to reignite her artistic side, the side she had ignored for so long it had stopped seeking her attention.

She justified her intentions to re-energize herself as a way to re-energize her business but somewhere deep down she knew it was more than that. It was a way to rekindle the sense of freedom that her art had always provided and that lately she'd felt was missing.

She had been told so many times that art was a distraction from the things that truly mattered, and that she needed to be able to be able to support herself as an independent woman who didn't need a man, that she had internalized the message to the point of no return. Only recently did she realize that she had *become* a successful woman who was more than capable of supporting herself and, dammit, she missed making art.

The open space on either side of the highway rolled by in striking green contrast to the gray, steel backdrop of the city she was used to.

She needed something to get her out of work mode and into week-by-herself-summer-vacation mode. Music had never let her down before and the diversion of song lyrics seemed like the best way to relax while she finished the drive to the Faraway Inn, the family-run bed and breakfast, in a small town called Hazelton, at the western end of the state. Though she was more of a classical music aficionado, her assistant's love of country music had started to rub off on her and classic country felt like the perfect soundtrack to a bright, warm, sunny July afternoon.

Not normally a Jimmy Buffett fan, "Margaritaville" was one of those songs she couldn't resist singing along with, so when it started playing through the Harman Kardon sound system of her new Mercedes, Victoria clicked up the volume, put down the windows, and since there was nobody around to hear her, she let loose and sang along.

She clicked the volume up another couple notches and unexpectedly felt a deep connection with Buffett's broken-hearted beach bum as he finally came to the realization that his dire situation was most likely self-inflicted. Probably a little too close to home. She took a sip from her water bottle and clicked over to the classic rock channel. A woman could never go wrong with a little old school Bon Jovi to keep her company.

Even belting out "Livin' on a Prayer" as loud as she could wasn't enough to keep her mind distracted from thoughts of what was happening back in Boston. Her fingers itched to call her assistant, Paige, and find out how things were going and maybe give her a bit of grief for convincing Victoria to embark on this self-reflection vacation. "Tell yourself it will benefit the company if you have to," Paige had said. "But just go and relax and practice making art while you learn to take some deep breaths." Luckily, the GPS stopped her from dialing when its AI voice instructed her to get off at the next exit, toward Hazelton.

About fifteen minutes later she found herself driving through the idyllic town, slowing down to take in the utter charm of the place. Wide streets, with ample parking, were lined with diners, a gas station, a small movie theater, and at least three different restaurants, along with an array of gift shops, a bakery and, much to her delight, a sign pointing up a side street to a chocolatier. That quintessential New

England hallmark, a white wood clapboard church, sat at the far end of the street, overlooking the downtown area.

Just after the center of town, a sign pointed north, indicating the direction to the Hazelton Art Museum and Gallery. An empty feeling settled into her stomach when she realized she'd be going that way tomorrow to see what, if anything, remained of her art skills.

"You're just hungry," she said to herself, rationalizing away the spark of fear as evidence of the fact that it was three o'clock and she still hadn't eaten lunch. She stopped looking around the town and continued driving until she arrived at 324 Benson Drive, The Faraway Inn.

The inn itself looked as if it belonged in a fairy tale. Her tight grip on the steering wheel eased slightly as she took in the old, two-story, safflower yellow Victorian with white-trimmed windows, sitting at the end of a long, gravel driveway. The deep front porch wrapped around the side of the house and was surrounded by plants in an explosion of colors and textures. Even the wooden sign had been painted in complimentary colors in an elegant script. She half expected a troupe of fairies, or whatever term one would use to name a collection of fairies, to rise from the flower beds as she watched.

Once she stepped out of the car, everything about her surroundings was different enough to feel slightly uncomfortable, including the way the air smelled. There weren't a lot of places to get the fresh cut grass smell in the city, but there was no way to avoid it out in the hinterlands of Hazelton. She inhaled a deep breath, determined to force herself to slow down, take in everything the area had to offer, and enjoy her birthday renaissance week.

Victoria hauled her suitcase out of the trunk, set her weekend bag on top of it then wheeled it across the driveway toward the front door of her home away from home for the next seven days.

Aaron

People watching without being recognized was a hobby Aaron Price had developed during years touring the country when he needed some down time away from the chaos of life as a musician on the road. In the past, a hat and sunglasses were all the disguise he needed to avoid detection from all but the most hardcore fans, but as years went on even those became less of a necessity and more of a habit.

He'd been at the Faraway for a few days already and had yet to see anyone who piqued his interest in any way other than as a casual observer. And then a most intriguing woman exited a black Mercedes, her hair a mess, as though she drove with the windows down instead of using the air conditioning, wearing a knee-length dress printed with large flowers. Her hips swayed as she strode across the driveway, pulling her giant wheeled suitcase behind her. Those hips piqued his interest almost as much as the cleavage on display at the top of her dress.

From his seat in the hammock swing under the giant maple tree, Aaron watched the woman walk, listened to the slapping sound her sandals made against her feet with each step she took, and an easy smile worked its way across his face. He looked back at the Mercedes to see if there was anyone else getting out of it, but it was still. Perhaps her companion would be meeting her later. Or perhaps she would be staying by herself. Odd but not unheard of. He himself was doing exactly that after all.

Years of this hobby helped him get an idea of a person simply by observing them without having to interact. Unless he chose to. Something about the bombshell approaching the front door of his sort of, almost inn told him he had just chosen to. Whether it was the way she walked, tall and with purpose, even though she was entering the most restful place he'd ever been, or the way she carried herself, shoulders back, full of confidence, he didn't know. Most likely it was a good deal of both. Either way, he was interested enough to leave the comfort of the fabric swing and follow her into the house.

Not wanting to intrude or appear as if he was eavesdropping, though he was one hundred percent eavesdropping, he walked across the large sitting room to the side table that the innkeepers set up every afternoon with two coffee urns and a plate of homemade cookies; today was chocolate chip.

The woman from the Mercedes stood on the customer side of the counter, across from Hattie, one half of the older couple who owned the Faraway.

Years spent traveling the world with his rock band, Undercover Angel, as well as his second career as a record producer, had him crossing paths with all manner of people, from the easiest of easy going, to insanely high strung, to entirely unlikable, and everywhere in between. But Hattie and her husband, Mitch, were genuinely decent people and two of the hardest workers he'd had the pleasure of meeting.

The work required to run a place like the Faraway was no joke, and it quickly became apparent why the older couple were eager to sell.

Hattie welcomed the new woman with her customary ear-to-ear smile, pointing out the amenities of the room, the map of local restaurants and attractions, and of course, the table of coffee and cookies where Aaron currently stood filling his cup and wrapping a cookie in a napkin.

"Thank you," the woman said, taking the map from Hattie. Her voice was strong, but not loud. It had a pleasant sound and he wondered what it sounded like when she laughed. "I have to tell you," she continued. "Your inn is absolutely spectacular. The grounds are gorgeous and—" she looked around the room, making brief eye contact with him before she returned her attention to Hattie, "the building itself is just so beautiful. It makes me feel like I'm in a fairy tale."

In usual Hattie fashion, she blushed and thanked the woman profusely. "Okay, Miss Lathrop, here is the key to your room. You'll be staying in Room 4, which is up the stairs, left around the banister, last door on the right."

Aaron knew the inn was intermittently booked for the week, though he had no idea which rooms were assigned to which guests. A warm pleasure traveled through his body when he learned that the Mercedes woman, Miss Lathrop, was staying in the room across the hall from his own.

"You can leave your bags at the bottom of the stairs, and I'll have Mitch bring them up for you in just a few minutes," Hattie added as Miss Lathrop stepped away from the counter.

"That's all right," she said. "I can certainly carry them up one flight."

Self-reliant? Stubborn? Or just polite? He couldn't read the woman's motivation from the tone of her voice, but he knew one way to find out.

As she approached the stairs, Aaron met her there. "May I?" he asked, nodding toward her large suitcase.

Victoria

She'd known he'd been watching her since she pulled into the driveway, yet she was still shocked by how obvious he was by approaching her as she attempted to go to her room. She tried to tell herself that she'd only noticed him because he was out there by himself, and not because he was so incredibly good-looking that she had to do a double take to make sure he wasn't some kind of celebrity.

The hat and the glasses made that hard to do, but now that they stood face-to-face, no more hat or glasses, he was still extremely good looking, though she didn't recognize him as anyone famous.

What she couldn't do, however, was let him carry her suitcase up the stairs for her. First, she was more than capable of carrying it by herself, and second, this was her week to relax and focus on herself; classes to take, books to read, the chance to see if any of her creative ability had stayed intact after so many years of squashing it down. The one thing she didn't need was to get sidetracked by a handsome stranger five minutes after walking in the door.

"I've got it," she said, hanging her small bag over one shoulder, then lifting the suitcase from the rustic hardwood floor. "But thank you anyway." She had one foot on the bottom step when he spoke again.

"I really don't mind," he said. "I'm going that way anyhow and I wouldn't feel right letting you carry that while all I have is a coffee and a cookie."

He held her gaze while she scrambled for a reason to keep saying no, until she remembered she didn't need a reason. "No, thank you," she said. "I've already told you I've got it." She took another step. "Enjoy your cookie," she said over her shoulder.

To her surprise he began walking right beside her. She threw him a questioning look.

"I've already told you I'm going up to my room," he said with a smile, and she couldn't help but wonder how much money he'd spent on dental work. His teeth were white and straight and damn-near perfect. They matched the handsomeness of his face, his hazel eyes that leaned a bit toward green. His slightly graying hair, that on anyone else would have looked like he was overdue for a trim, somehow fit this man to a T.

"I'm Aaron," he said then looked down at his hands, a coffee in one and a cookie in the other, as if trying to figure out how to shake her hand. With a quick shrug he shoved the cookie into his mouth, wiped his hand on his jeans then stuck it out for a shake.

"Victoria," she said, and against her better judgment, put her hand into his. He had a firm grip without being aggressive and she liked the way it felt. She'd shaken a lot of hands with a lot of people over the years. Being an entrepreneur was nothing if not a social job, but she'd never quite enjoyed a simple handshake the way she just had. "Nice to meet you."

He swallowed down his cookie and once again flashed that smile, making her belly all fluttery and she knew if she let down her guard even for a minute, her carefully crafted week could be entirely unraveled before she knew the thread had been pulled. "Now that I have a free hand, I can take that for you," he said and grabbed her suitcase and started up the stairs.

Briefly stunned into inaction by his gesture, Victoria jogged up the steps behind him and when they reached the top, took hold of the suitcase handle. "Thank you," she said. "I can get it from here."

She felt his eyes on her as she rounded the railing and headed toward her room, so she turned, caught him in the act, though he didn't appear ashamed at all, and gave him her best *Go away, I'm not interested* face.

Rather than take the hint, he said, "Will I see you at dinner? Tonight's Mitch's specialty; burgers on the grill with corn on the cob."

"I don't think so," she replied. "I don't eat red meat."

After she had taken a few more steps toward her room, he said, "How about pizza?" He was quiet for a moment before he said, "Around seven o'clock?"

Victoria didn't know whether to laugh or tell this guy to go away, or both. Her opinion of him fluctuated from handsome and charming, to extremely pushy, and back again. Despite his charm and incredibly sexy body—tall, broad, and trim—the thought of having dinner with a stranger and having to be 'on' after a long afternoon of driving wasn't in her plans. What she really wanted to do was take a long soaking bath, put on some comfortable clothes, and read a book on the couch in the cozy living room she'd briefly passed through.

"It's a very nice offer," she said. "But I think I'm going to pass. Thank you, though." She turned the key in the door lock, let herself inside, then locked it behind her without looking back and potentially giving him another chance to continue the conversation.

A thrill wound its way through her body as she thought about the idea of attracting a man like Aaron. Judging strictly by the surface observations she could make, he seemed friendly, if a tad pushy, but he didn't give off stalker vibes or anything. He was obviously good looking. And he had clearly expressed an interest in her. She turned back to check through the door's peephole to see if he was still there, but he was gone from the hallway.

Had it been so long that simply flirting with a handsome guy had her middle feeling all squishy? Quickly doing the math, she realized it had been almost eight months since her last date, and closer to a year since she'd actually had sex.

Blowing out a frustrated breath, she sent off a quick text to Paige.

> *Got here a little while ago. You were right. It's amazing.*

>> *Glad you made it! Have fun! We've got everything under control here. Enjoy your week and make something amazing!*

Victoria hesitated then quickly typed a reply.

> *I already had a guy ask me out to dinner!*

>> *You're wearing the floral dress that shows off your boobs, aren't you?*

Victoria looked down at her chest then at her reflection in the mirror above the dark wood bureau. The dress really did flatter her figure, with an emphasis on her chest.

> *Yes you think that's why?*

> *Duh I told you it was hot!! Where are you going for dinner?*

> *I said no.*

> *Not your type?*

> *Extremely attractive, perfect teeth, nice smile, great body, and a firm handshake. I think he is my type.*

Her stomach flipped as that idea took hold. But then reality reminded her that not only had she just met the man, but she also had her own plans for her time in the Berkshires, so she definitely made the right call in saying no to his invitation.

> *Victoria! I know you need some creative time but don't forget it's still a vacation!*

> *It's OK to lighten up and enjoy yourself! As long as he's not a creep you should totally go!*

> *Don't be afraid to have a little fun.*

> *Maybe some vacay sex??*

Vacation sex? With a complete stranger? They had talked for a few minutes, so maybe he wasn't a complete stranger, but still...

She ignored the warm tingling in her girl parts and snapped a couple photos of the room, with its cottage vibe, including the white claw foot tub with the over sized fluffy towel on the small wicker table beside it.

> *I don't think so. Gotta go. Need to soak in this tub right now.*

Aaron

He wasn't surprised she'd said no to dinner; he was surprised that she hadn't put up more of a fight against him carrying her suitcase up the stairs. He'd expected her to take it out of his hands as soon as he grabbed it, but she didn't. She had hurried to catch up with him, but it wasn't until he put the suitcase down on the landing that she'd taken it back from him. And that look... she'd clearly tried to scare him off with that scowl. Except it was so fucking cute it had the exact opposite effect and only served to energize his efforts to get her as interested in him as he was in her.

Once she'd disappeared into her room, he'd turned around and gone back downstairs to the inn's game room. It was small, set back from the main living room, and it had a polished, rustic wood counter around the perimeter with wooden bar stools tucked beneath it. There was a tall rack of board games in one corner and a small bookshelf that had been stocked with a variety of paperbacks in another. The crown jewel of the room was the green felt-topped pool table in the center of the floor.

He wasn't in the mood to shoot pool by himself, so he grabbed a well-worn copy of *Salem's Lot* and headed out to the backyard. The sun shone from a brilliant blue sky and the crystal-clear pool beckoned him, but he resisted the temptation to take a quick dip. He could only deal with one temptation at a time.

One outdoor couch was shaded by an umbrella, so he sat there to flip through the book as he waited for Victoria to come back downstairs. About an hour, yet only about ten pages of *Salem's Lot* later, he looked up to see her walking through the French doors out to the backyard.

Gone were the flowery sundress and wind-whipped hair; in their place was a pair of black bike shorts and a gray tee shirt, her wet hair hanging straight down her back. She looked relaxed and he wondered if she knew how well it suited her.

"Hey," she said as she walked out onto the stone patio. Looking around the landscaped backyard, an appreciative smile grew across her face. "Wow, it's just as beautiful out here as it is in there."

Even more beautiful now, he thought. "Hattie and Mitch are amazing, aren't they?" he said, closing the book and resting it on the seat beside him. "Mitch does all of this himself."

She sat in the chair to his right, one leg crossed over the other, both knees pointed his way. All good signs. "Any chance you changed your mind about having dinner with me tonight?"

"Seriously?"

"Yeah, seriously. Why not?"

"Because I already said no, for starters." Her fingers drummed the arms of her chair as she stared, waiting for his reply.

"Fair enough," he said, but was unwilling to let her off that easily. "But I think you're making a mistake."

Her eyes popped open, and she let out a soft chuckle. "Is that so?"

"Oh yeah," he said. "Big mistake."

After uncrossing her legs and then recrossing them in the other direction, she leaned back in her chair and scanned him from head to toe, telling him with one look that she was interested. "And why is that?" she said.

He was having a good time pushing her, and he knew by the fact that she hadn't told him to fuck off yet, a little more convincing might finally get a yes out of her. "Because I am a very nice guy. I have impeccable manners. And if that's not enough to convince you, I very much tend to the generous side."

Her lips parted slightly, and her eyes locked onto his. "Oh?" she said. "In what way?"

With one tiny gesture she had moved from casual flirting to borderline seduction. Flicking a glance at her full lips before returning to those watching eyes, he said, "In all the ways, of course."

She was quiet for a few seconds before her lips tipped into a teasing smile. "You're awfully persistent, do you know that?"

"I've been told," he said with a laugh. "How about this? You strike me as a competitive person. How about I play you for the chance to take you out?" It wasn't a tactic he would have used on most other women but something about Victoria told him she'd have a hard time declining an opportunity to compete.

A wider smile spread across her face. "What kind of competition did you have in mind?" She looked around the yard. "There's a badminton net over there but I don't see any rackets."

"Do you play pool?"

Her eyebrows pulled together in a look of confusion. "Pool?"

"Yeah," he said. "You haven't seen the game room?"

Leaning forward in her chair, she placed her hands on her knees. "I have not seen the game room. But I have to admit I'm intrigued."

"Wait, you're intrigued by the game room but not by my invitation to dinner? I'm not sure how I feel about that," he teased. "But if it means you'll play me for the chance to take you out, I'll show you where it is."

Her smile morphed back into a smirk, and he wondered if maybe she was a pool shark, meaning his brilliant idea was about to backfire on him.

"I haven't played in a few years," she said. "How often do you play?"

He had to think for a minute. "Before you showed up this afternoon, I played a quick practice round. Before that, it was about five years ago." He didn't want to lose his chance, so he decided to keep pushing. "Unless your skills are too rusty, and you're afraid you'll lose? Or are you secretly afraid you'll win?"

Without any hesitation, she stood and said, "You rack, I break."

Victoria

Afraid to lose. She couldn't remember the last time she'd been afraid to lose. But afraid to win was a whole other emotion she wasn't prepared to face, nor was she prepared to answer when Aaron brought it up. Would she be upset, or even mildly disappointed, if she won and they didn't go out to dinner? Maybe, but even so, there was no way she would throw a game. She would've impaled herself on her pool cue first.

As Aaron racked the balls, she chalked up the end of her cue.

"First round for practice?" he asked as he removed the rack, leaving a neat triangle of brightly colored balls in the center of the table. "Or you feeling lucky?"

"What's the matter? Afraid you can't keep up?" She flicked a glance over her shoulder right before she leaned over and lined up her cue. After a few practice strokes she let go with her breaking shot. The multicolored balls scattered all over the table, the purple number four ball sinking into the far corner pocket.

"Nice shot," he said, though his face didn't give away any of what he was feeling or thinking.

"Thanks," she said, then lined up and took aim at the blue number two ball but failed to sink it.

After that, it was all Aaron. Shot after shot, one striped ball after another, until he finally sunk the black eight ball in the side pocket, ending the game almost as quickly as it had begun.

"Only one practice game this afternoon, huh?" she said as he slid his cue back into the rack on the wall.

He grinned over his shoulder. "It came back to me pretty fast." He faced her, resting his body against the counter. "What kind of pizza do you like?"

"How about the best two out of three?" she said, completely irritated with how that game turned out and needing to try to prove herself to him.

"I will gladly play you again, but not for dinner. I won that one fair and square. If you want to play another game to see who buys dessert, then I'm all in." His arms were folded over his chest, but his demeanor was nothing but relaxed.

If she paid any attention to the swarming butterflies in her belly, she would have to acknowledge to herself that she was intrigued at the prospect of having dinner with Aaron, but she still couldn't resist the challenge of another game. "I'll rack, you break this time. Loser buys dessert." She rounded up the balls and assembled them in the triangle. "Oh, I should probably tell you, I don't like pizza, so we'll have to find somewhere else to go."

Aaron's eyes went wide. "What? No burgers. No pizza. Mind if I ask what you do like to eat?"

"Pretty much anything except burgers and pizza." Turning her back toward his shocked face, she removed the wooden triangle from the table, handed Aaron his cue and stood back to wait for her turn.

The second game was a little less lopsided than the first, but Victoria still came out on the losing side.

"I guess that was two out of three," he said as he replaced his cue on the rack for the second time. "How about Mexican food? There's a great little place downtown. Hattie told me about it when I first got here. Food was amazing and the service was excellent."

It was only dinner, so nothing to get overly worked up about. She was only in town for a week, and she had no idea what Aaron's plans were, so there couldn't be any expectations on either side, aside from eating a meal together, Paige's advice for some vacation sex notwithstanding.

Still, he was an almost complete stranger, and a woman couldn't be too careful. "Fine," she said. "But I don't know you from Adam, so I'm driving and we're taking my car."

When he smiled, the outside edges of his eyes crinkled, and it was sexy as hell. "Wouldn't have guessed otherwise."

Aaron

E xactly as he'd expected, Victoria was a good driver, bold without being aggressive, though how anyone could be aggressive surrounded by the natural, calming beauty of the Berkshires was beyond him. Either way, he found right from the start that he enjoyed being with her.

All his years of people watching gave him clues to her, but it turned out she was fairly open as they talked over dinner. Choosing to sit outside in the open-air dining area behind the restaurant, the conversation flowed easily between them, the only exception being his response when she asked what he did for a living.

It was the question he hated the most, but it was, naturally enough, the first question people asked him. In his younger years, most everyone he met already knew who he was, so it wasn't much of an issue. The real problem came with trying to figure out who liked him for himself and who liked him simply because he was Aaron Price, Undercover Angel co-founder and lead guitarist.

It mattered less with the guys he met, but the women were a little trickier. More than once he'd been hurt by women who pretended to care about him but only cared about what he could do for them, how much money he would spend on them, and who he could help them meet.

His more recent answer, record producer, wasn't technically a lie and it usually kept the conversation steered in a way he could control. Undercover Angel had broken up for good a little over five years ago, and slowly, over time, fewer and fewer people recognized him. Every now and again people would double take when they saw him, but overall, he enjoyed the peace his relative anonymity brought back to him.

Victoria appeared to have no idea who he was, so he ventured to give her a variation of the truth. "Musician," he said.

"Tough way to make a living, I bet," Victoria said as she ate a bite of her chicken queso bowl.

He liked this woman. He liked the way she looked at him and was so quick to laugh with him. He liked her confidence and the way she carried herself. He also really liked that she had no idea who the hell he was. Stifling a laugh, he said, "Not as hard as you might think."

Her single raised eyebrow told him she was definitely curious about his comment, so he changed the subject back to her. "How about you? How do you earn your living?"

Her face brightened instantly. "I started my own company about ten years ago," she said. "We manage web sites and social media presence for companies that don't want to do it themselves. A lot of big companies have departments dedicated to it, but a lot of smaller ones will contract out. So, for example, people like Hattie and Mitch are super busy with the day-to-day work of running the inn. They could contract with us to run their web site and social pages, and do the work of trying to get people out here through those channels."

The whole time she talked she didn't eat because her hands were completely involved in the conversation. And he knew exactly which company he'd hire to run the social media side of things if and when he ended up buying the Faraway.

Keeping the conversation focused on her, he said, "Sounds like a lot of work. How big's your company?"

"Right now, there are twenty of us and, yeah, it's a whole lot of work." She lowered her eyes to the table briefly. "I almost didn't come out here this week, but my assistant pretty much told me she was going to have the locks changed and then change all my passwords if I didn't go away and relax for a while." When she laughed it had a tinge of guilt in it. "So, here I am!"

She definitely came across as an in-charge, work-like-hell kind of person, so her tone of voice was telling. "Not much of a vacationer I take it?"

With a quick shrug, she said, "Not really." Sitting upright, she pushed her shoulders back and continued. "My company is really important to me. I've worked my ass off to get it where it is today. Stepping away, even for a week, just never worked out for me." Removing her napkin from her lap, she twisted it like a rope before placing it on the table beside her plate. Her shoulders slumped slightly before she said, "If I'm being honest, though, I'm getting a little burned out. My sleep isn't great anymore, no matter how much I work out, or meditate, or whatever."

She huffed out another laugh that held a hint of something else. Shame? Embarrassment? Guilt? Catching his gaze again, she said, "I've been getting a little hard to work with and my assistant was right in kicking me out of the office for the week." Then she dropped her eyes to the twisted-up napkin and shrugged one shoulder.

"You're lucky to have someone like that," he said. Although he felt like the lucky one since she happened to pick the same week at the inn that he was staying there.

"No doubt," she said, looking back up at him. "She's unbelievable. There's no way I'd be where I am today without Paige."

"That's awesome," he said. "So, what are your Paige-approved plans for your vacation? Lots of relaxing and swimming and things like that?"

Her brow furrowed and she fidgeted in her seat. In a low voice, she said, "Just some art stuff."

Angling his head to catch her eye again, he said, "What kind of art stuff? Are you an artist?"

"No, not really. At least not anymore. I used to be. But I kind of miss it. I'm just taking a couple classes. Nothing too big." Waving her hand, she caught the server's attention and the young man quickly approached with their check. To Aaron she said, "What do you think? Want to get out of here?"

There was definitely more to that story, but he didn't push her to talk. Not yet. Maybe once they'd gotten to know each other a little better she'd volunteer it.

As they strolled down the quaint main street through town, Victoria said, "You said Hattie recommended this place when you got to the inn. How long have you been there?"

"Since the middle of last week," he said. "I'll be here through the middle of next week. I'm trying to get the feel of the area, the inn, the whole vibe out here. I've never spent any real time in Massachusetts so I'm figuring out if I'd like it or not."

"What do you think of it so far?"

"So far so good," he said, being intentionally vague. "It's certainly beautiful here, that's for sure." The way she smiled before she looked away let him know that she understood his compliment had been directed at her.

"It's a great state to live in," she said. "I've lived here my whole life but I'm ashamed to admit I've never ventured this far west." She stopped walking, looked up one side of the street and down the other. "It is just so charming out here. Look at that place," she said, pointing to a local gift shop they approached. "I'll bet they have the cutest things in there." She looked at the posted hours and frowned. "They're already closed. But I am totally coming back here before I go home."

They kept walking, avoiding several planters overflowing with vibrant flowers as well as several other couples coming and going from the local restaurants.

"What made you want to come to Massachusetts anyway?" Victoria asked.

He was glad to switch to a topic he was comfortable discussing that had nothing to do with his work or his past. "My daughter's interested in owning a bed and breakfast, but she needs some help with the initial investment. I've done a bit of research and found that the Faraway is going on the market soon."

"Whoa," she said. "That's pretty huge. How old is your daughter?"

"Almost twenty-five," he said. She had been primarily raised by her mother, who turned out to be one of those women who was interested in him for his money and what he could do for her. Despite their frequent time apart while she was growing up, he and his daughter had been able to forge a strong relationship. While there was no way to make up for any of the lost time, helping her with her biggest dream was as good an attempt as any.

"But I'm not sure she understands the amount of work it's going to be without someone to run the business with her," he said. "While I'm extremely confident in my daughter's abilities, I think it would be too much for any one person on their own."

"I'd say so," she said. "That's why you're here for a couple of weeks. You're doing the business side of the scouting for her?"

"Pretty much. I have nothing going on at the moment, so I thought I'd help her out." He was in between producing projects and wasn't in a big hurry to take on another one, even though he had artists waiting to work with him. It seemed that, similarly to Victoria, he was starting to burn out and needed a break.

"I have to ask; what made her want to run a B and B?" she said. "That's kind of a huge decision at such a young age."

He'd had the exact same thought when Alyssa had first mentioned it but the more she talked about it, the more intrigued he'd become. And if it didn't work out, all they had to do was sell the place and call it a learning experience.

"Pretty sure she's seen too many romance movies and is expecting a never-ending stream of eligible singles who hate Christmas to come through the front door so she can prove them wrong by fixing them up with all the other Christmas-hating singles at the inn. She's always been a romantic like that," he said with a laugh.

Victoria's eyes narrowed a fraction as she slowed her pace and held his gaze.

"What?" he asked, unable to read her expression.

"Trying to figure you out."

"Don't try too hard," he said, afraid that she might. "Come on, let's keep going."

The conversation hit a companionable silence as they each checked out the different storefronts they passed. Looking ahead he saw a hanging sign in the shape of an ice cream cone. "Want to stop for a scoop?" he asked.

Looking sheepish, she said, "I should probably tell you I don't like ice cream either."

"Oh, come on. Who doesn't like ice cream? Are you sure you're even American?" He bumped her shoulder with his own, causing her to laugh. "Please tell me you at least like baseball and apple pie."

"I love baseball; Red Sox all the way. I don't like apple pie, but I'll eat pecan pie until I'm sick. Does that count?"

Aaron had become a de facto Yankees fan when he moved to New York a few years ago, though his true sporting love was hockey. "I'll accept pecan pie, but the Red Sox?"

Stopping short, she planted her hands on her hips and jutted her chin out at him. "Watch it, mister. Born and raised in this state and I'm a third generation Sox fan." Her eyebrows lifted, challenging him to keep arguing.

Her carefully controlled exterior had started to come down a bit and he had to work to keep his hands to himself. The urge to reach out and hold her hand or touch her hair was real, and, he was well aware, way too soon.

Seeing her standing there so defiantly had him wondering how much of that was who she really was and how much was a show. If and when he got her into bed, he was fairly certain that controlling nature of hers would go right out the window. And he couldn't wait to show her how good it would feel to let go and let someone else be in charge for once.

"Good enough," he said with a laugh, hands raised in a gesture of surrender. "There's a chocolate shop around the block that way. Think you can find something you like in there?"

"There's zero chance I won't."

Victoria

H er day started the way her days always started, before sunrise, and she tiptoed down to the kitchen to brew a cup of coffee, which she took with her to the front porch. The morning air was cool, and she snuggled deeper into her sweatshirt to keep the slight chill at bay.

As she sat on the porch swing in the slowly gathering dawn, legs stretched out before her, Victoria breathed the clean, cool air deep into her lungs. Dinner with Aaron the night before had given her plenty to think about as she watched the dark horizon start to glimmer in shades of yellow and orange.

Her journal sat, closed, beside her after she had spent some time noting all the things about Aaron that she had enjoyed—good manners, a handsome face, easy conversation, a body that she wanted to climb like a jungle gym—as well as the things that could potentially be considered issues—he didn't live in Massachusetts, they would only be together for a week. But the real deal breaker was his occupation as a musician.

Growing up with a single mom, certain skills and abilities were prized above others. For her daughters, Elizabeth Lathrop wanted successful lives and careers, and successful partners to go along with those things. Victoria and her sister, Missy, were discouraged from pursuing "frivolous" pursuits like art and music in favor of more "level-headed" things like web design and debate club. And horror of horrors was when Missy made the mistake of wanting to date a drummer when she was in high school. Victoria wasn't sure if Missy really liked the guy or if she only dated him to drive their mother crazy.

But Victoria wasn't in high school anymore and she had honored her mother's wishes and become a successful entrepreneur. So why was it still so hard to take Aaron seriously as a potential match? Was it her own hesitation, or her mother's, niggling around in her mind?

A few minutes after the sun came up, she heard the door open behind her. Thinking it was Aaron, she tucked her journal under her leg and turned to see him. Rather than Aaron, she saw Mitch, dressed in dark jeans and a green polo shirt, walking out with a bowl and a pair of scissors in his hands.

Fixing a smile onto her face to hide the pinch of disappointment, she pulled her shoulders back and sat up taller as the screen door closed behind him. "Morning, Mitch," she said, so he wouldn't be startled when he realized she was out there.

"Oh, Miss Lathrop, nice to see a friendly face at this hour." His smile warmed her as he stood beside the swing and looked out at the rising sun. "Beautiful day on tap," he said, jutting his chin toward the sunrise. "Got big plans to do any sightseeing or you just relaxing by the pool today?"

Why was she hesitant to confess to taking an art class? Hell, the art scene was one of the area's biggest selling points on every travel website she used. There were museums and art galleries everywhere she looked. Surely, she was not the first person staying at the Faraway to indulge their creative side. Still, admitting it out loud felt disloyal to the strait-laced businessperson she understood herself to be. And, as odd as it was, to the well-intentioned mother who had raised her.

"I'm not terribly good at relaxing, Mitch. But I'm supposed to be taking a class over at the Hazelton Art Museum this afternoon. I guess, maybe, I could do a little sightseeing before that," she said.

"That's a nice place, the art museum. Hattie and I have been there a few times over the years for different exhibits. You'll have a good time there. Nice folks." He ambled down the steps and disappeared from view as he knelt to work in the garden.

As an admirer of the inn's landscaping, she couldn't resist a chance to see Mitch in action. "Whatcha doing?" she asked, leaning forward to watch him work.

"Oh, just snipping some herbs for Hattie to use when she makes breakfast. A little thyme and rosemary for baked eggs and some oregano and basil for the roasted potatoes. And then I try to find a nice flower or two to bring in for her. She loves them and they make her smile."

Victoria clutched a hand to her heart. "Mitch," she said. "That might be the sweetest thing I've ever heard."

Mitch laughed and shook his head. "If you say so."

She stood from the swing and leaned over the railing to watch him work. "How do you know what to cut and how much to cut off without killing them? I wasn't gifted with a green thumb so anyone who can grow plants like this is part wizard as far as I'm concerned."

With the enthusiasm of a teacher who loved their subject, Mitch motioned for her to join him by the herb garden, handed her the scissors. "Rosemary is fairly strong, so she doesn't need a lot. Why don't you cut off a few sprigs for me?"

More than anything she wanted to take the scissors and snip a few sprigs, only she had no idea which one was rosemary. Sensing her hesitation, Mitch pointed to a plant that looked vaguely like an unkempt Christmas tree, with its little evergreen branches looking like a green pompom. "Pick a sturdy branch, then snip the top few inches off and toss them in the bowl."

The first cut felt good, like she too could grow plants like Mitch. It didn't matter that she had no idea which plant was which. The pungent scent of the plant clung to her fingers, and she made a mental note that she wanted to try growing some rosemary when she made it back home.

Thyme and oregano were next, and she followed his instructions for snipping just above a set of leaves to encourage more growth. "Make sure you leave enough of the stem to help support those little leaves when they start to get big," he said. "Nice work," he added as she did as he instructed.

Far and away, basil was her favorite. The familiar, almost lemony smell of the broad leaves brought to mind her favorite caprese appetizers; cherry tomatoes, mozzarella cheese, and a fresh basil leaf on a small skewer, drizzled in balsamic glaze. When her belly gurgled Mitch laughed. "Just wait until you smell her cooking with all this," he said. "It's a wonder I don't weigh a ton with the way she cooks."

The way Mitch spoke about his wife, though not particularly romantic, still evoked a sense of longing in her heart that she'd been avoiding for a long time.

Once she got the hang of it, she marveled at how easy and how fun it was to care for the various plants. Once the bowl overflowed with fresh herbs, Mitch picked up the bowl and the scissors, along with a large blossom of tiny blue flowers he'd picked for Hattie. "Hydrangeas are her favorite and they look real pretty when they dry," he said as he headed back up the stairs.

Sitting back down on the swing, she picked up her journal and made a few notes. She tried to write down as many things as she could remember that Mitch had told her about each of the plants but knew she'd probably forgotten a bunch.

Then, without giving it too much thought, she rose from the swing, went back down to sit in front of the herb garden and sketched the rosemary plant. It was terrible; barely recognizable as a plant, let alone a rosemary bush. The only thing it had going for it was the fact that it was done by her own hand. Her heart ached knowing how poorly her art class was certainly going to go.

Perhaps the whole idea of a creative vacation was as ridiculous as she originally thought it would be. Maybe the best thing would be to cancel her classes and take a nice, week-long swim instead.

Aaron

Her quiet nature while she was paying attention to Mitch's instructions intrigued him. The smile on her face as she cut herbs and then her furrowed brow as he explained something to her that Aaron couldn't hear, showed that she was a woman who appreciated what she was learning.

He'd gotten up early, like most days, to get as much enjoyment out of his day as possible. After fixing his coffee, he intended to head out to the front porch swing but had stopped and watched through the window instead. He found more enjoyment watching their interactions than he'd expected.

Victoria, in yoga pants, a sweatshirt, and flip flops, with her hair in a high ponytail, worked carefully to cut plants while Mitch showed her what to do. The look of concentration on her face as she worked, and then her pride at a job well done, hit him squarely, yet unexpectedly, in the heart.

Mitch straightened to come back inside, so Aaron retreated to the living room couch to finish drinking his coffee.

"Oh, hey, Aaron," Mitch said as he came back through the front door. "Beautiful morning out there," he added with a wink, then disappeared into the kitchen to help Hattie get started on breakfast.

Had Mitch seen him through the window? He didn't think so, but it was possible.

He refilled his cup and brought it out to the front porch. Looking down toward the garden he saw Victoria sitting cross-legged in front of the plants, her elbows resting on her knees and her face resting in her hands. She blew out a hard breath, slapped one hand onto the ground and pushed herself up to standing.

"You alright down there?" he asked and took a sip of coffee. "Anything I can do to help?"

She stuffed a small pink notebook under her arm and climbed up the steps. "I'm fine," she said, then walked past him and plopped into her previous spot on the swing. She tossed the notebook off to the side where it landed with a slap on the wood planks.

Apparently, her lesson with Mitch hadn't gone as smoothly as he'd seen from the window, or something else was bothering her. "Can I get you a refill on your coffee?"

Watery eyes looked up at him. "Really? You'd do that for me?"

"Of course I would. Cream and sugar?"

She nodded, handed him her empty mug then wiped her eyes on the cuffs of her sweatshirt sleeves.

When he came back with her coffee she was staring off into the distance, but he was glad to see she wasn't crying. "Mind if I sit?"

She scooted over and patted the seat next to her. "There's plenty of room."

"Everything OK?" he asked again as handed over her coffee.

She let out a little sigh. "Yeah, everything's alright. I'm just a little frustrated with myself."

So it had nothing to do with Mitch, which meant it might have had something to do with him. Treading carefully, he asked, "Want to talk about it? I might be able to help."

"I want to tell you it's really complicated, but it's not." Her lips pulled to one side in more of a grimace than a smile. "I guess I'm just a little confused right now," she said.

"Confused about what?" He wanted to ask if her confusion had anything to do with him, but he didn't want to come off as presumptuous.

"I told you I came out here to take some classes, right?"

He nodded, not sure what there was to be confused about.

She wrapped her arms around her midsection and let her head droop. Huffing out a small laugh, she said, "God, I don't even know you and I feel like I'm opening up to my therapist."

"It's all good," he said, placing his hand on her thigh. "Totally judgment free listener."

Her head lifted and she looked sideways at him before she rested her hand on top of his and gently squeezed his fingers. "Thanks." She was quiet for a few seconds before she said, "Do you think parental expectations can carry through into adulthood?" Quickly she said, "Like, the things you were allowed to do or encouraged to do somehow became your personality and it just sort of stuck. And now that you're trying to tap into something that's been neglected for so long, it somehow feels like a betrayal?"

He flipped his hand face up and twined his fingers with hers. "That's not something I have personally experienced, but I can certainly see how that could happen. My parents were completely on board with my music from the beginning. My mom was probably my biggest fan." He laughed. "She might still be."

"Don't misunderstand," Victoria said. "My mother only wanted the best for us. It's not like she was some overbearing tyrant or anything like that. She just struggled and worked so hard as a single mom after my dad left and she never wanted me or my sister to have to struggle the way she did. 'Always be able to support yourself,' was like an anthem in my house growing up. And anytime my father would show back up and add to the chaos, she would double down on making sure my sister and I were keeping good grades and doing the right activities."

She sighed deeply and Aaron felt her sorrow. "Which meant giving up on the ones that we loved. At least for me it did. My sister is three years younger, and she always sort of did her own thing." She chuckled. "But for me, that meant giving up the idea of studying art, which led to giving up on it all together."

He could logically understand what she said but emotionally he couldn't relate. Giving up music would be like giving up breathing. He couldn't do it and wouldn't do it, no matter who had asked. Even if Undercover Angel had stayed playing local bars and never made it to worldwide stadium tours, he would still live with a guitar within reach.

"There's no reason you can't start chasing that goal now, is there? It seems to me, you did exactly what your mother wanted, and you're more than capable of taking care of yourself. But what if taking care of yourself means going after a new goal? One that you put off for a long fucking time. Too long if you ask me."

Without speaking she reached down and grabbed her pink notebook from the floor, flipped open to a page with a pencil sketch of a plant, and placed it on his lap. "That," she said, pointing to the sketch. "That is what's left of my artistic ability. A sketch that looks like a bunch of sticks drawn by a third grader."

Knowing his own attempt at what she drew actually would have looked like it had been drawn by a third grader, he couldn't help but laugh. "You're kidding, right? I think this looks really good. It's certainly a whole lot better than anything I could've done." He liked holding her hand, so he reached out and took it in his own again. "When's the last time you drew anything?"

In a quiet voice she said, "About ten years ago or so. Around the same time I started my business."

"Then that makes this all the better," he said. "Because if I hadn't picked up a guitar in ten years, I can't even imagine the noise that'd come out of it." The thought of not touching a guitar in a decade brought physical pain to his stomach. He had no idea what it would sound like if he hadn't played in that long because it would never happen, but he wanted to make her feel better.

"Can I have this?" he asked, pointing to her sketch.

"What? Why the hell would you want a terrible sketch of a plant that I can't even grow?"

"I just like it," he said. "And beauty is in the eye of the beholder and all that, right?" When she nodded, he handed it back and said, "An artist always signs her work."

She chuckled as she took the book from him, then grabbed her pencil and signed her name in the bottom right corner before she ripped out the page and handed it to him.

"So, changing the subject entirely," he said. "Was Mitch teaching you everything he knows about gardening?"

"Hardly," she said. "I don't think even Mitch has enough patience for all that. But he did show me how to cut them so they'll grow more leaves, and he told me how to plant them and grow them in pots and how to tell if they have enough water and when to add fertilizer." She held up her pink notebook. "I tried to write down everything he told me but I'm sure I missed something." Smiling, she said, "I guess I'll have to Google whatever I can't remember."

"I've got to be honest with you," he said. "I never in a million years would have pegged you as a pink notebook kind of woman. Steel gray? Absolutely. But pink? Never. Nor could I have ever imagined you growing your own herbs."

She held a hand against her heart. "Ouch," she said. "That hurt."

"I didn't mean it to," he said. "It's just that the pink notebook and the herb gardening make a little more sense after what you just shared with me. It's kind of cool to see your outside match your inside, that's all."

He was at a distinct disadvantage because he was not about to share his own secret with her. It wasn't that he didn't trust her to know who he was, it was simply because his experience so far told him it would be better to leave that part of himself hidden and just enjoy the time they had together.

Victoria

T he charcoal was clumsy in her hand at first. But before long it started to come back to her. Not the medium of charcoal, that was new to her, but the way her hand moved over the paper, the way her brain began to relax as she focused on the image in front of her. For the first time in a long time, her actions weren't geared toward an end result, freeing her to focus on creativity for its own sake.

Putting the charcoal down, her stomach knotted as she stared at the mess on the once-white paper and realized maybe her artistic abilities would be better expressed through a different media, like sculpting. Or knitting. Or literally anything else besides charcoal.

Her shoulders relaxed though, as she looked around the large, open art room where the class was being held. The other students were hard at work creating their own, highly varied pieces. Several were cutting shapes with X-ACTO knives while another washed brushes in the sink. One older woman had accidentally created a beautiful abstract piece with tempera paint and India ink on watercolor paper, the black shadows of the ink giving the whole piece a nostalgic feel. It was energetic yet peaceful.

The one thing she noticed was that nobody made anything that looked like anyone else's work. It wasn't an assembly line of art, or a one-size-fits-all type of class, where everyone made a variation of the exact same thing. Looking down at her own paper, the urge to crumble it up and toss it in the trash faded and she began to see it in its own amateur light and tried to accept it as it was.

Maybe Aaron will like it, she thought. Not for the first time since she left the inn, she thought about Aaron. He told her he had plans to shadow Hattie and Mitch for the day to get a better understanding of what was involved in running the inn on a day-to-day basis. Still, she couldn't stop the bounce in her toes whenever she thought of him. She was enjoying her class, yet continually found herself checking the time.

A memory of her mother's reaction to Missy bringing her drummer-boyfriend home for dinner suddenly popped into her head and she had to cover her mouth with her hand to keep from laughing out loud and interrupting the Zen atmosphere of the art room. Her mother had been shocked, to say the least, and all but threw the boy out the door as soon as dinner was over. Once he was gone, the fireworks had started.

"Are you kidding me right now, Missy?" their mother had said. "Musicians are not marriage material, and you know that! You will be supporting his sorry ass for the rest of your life!"

"Jesus, I don't want to marry him, Mom, we're just dating!" Missy had yelled.

"Oh, right! Until you have to share him with every friggin' girl at his shows. By definition they're all womanizers. No way around it. You'll think you're special. He'll even tell you you're the only one. He will be lying to you! Musicians are the biggest liars on the planet." She'd clapped her hand for emphasis on every beat of her last sentence.

"OK, fine!" Missy had fired back, unsure how to combat their mother's 'logic.' "Then we'll just have sex, then, is that better? Is that what you want me to say? Because I'm not marrying him and I'm not breaking up with him, Mom!"

All these years later, and those familiar warnings from her upbringing rang through her mind as she entertained the idea of pursuing things with Aaron, eventually leading to the inevitable introductions to her family. She could only imagine how well that would go over.

Aaron

If Alyssa seriously wanted to make a go at this business, she would need to understand exactly what was involved in running a bed and breakfast. The amount of time and energy that went into running the inn wasn't small and after spending most of the day working with Hattie and Mitch, he had an even greater appreciation for the older couple and the amount of work involved than he already did.

Between the landscaping and pool maintenance outside and the housekeeping, laundry, and planning and prep before each meal inside, he was exhausted by the end of the day. As tired as he was, he wasn't too tired to have a glass of iced tea out by the pool. Sitting in his bathing suit with his aching feet stretched out in front of him, his attention was drawn by the noise of the door opening and then by the stunning beauty in the black, ruffled bikini walking through it. His mouth went dry, and he had to take an extra-long drink of iced tea before he could speak.

"How was your day?" he asked as Victoria dropped her towel and sunglasses onto the chair next to his. "Make some amazing art?"

"Something like that," she said with a grin, then looked at the pool. "But I really need to cool off before I'm ready to talk about it. Coming in?"

The sun had not yet started its descent, the air was heavy, hot, and humid, and a dip in the pool was exactly what he needed. Especially when that dip meant he could be closer to Victoria. "Absolutely."

Before he had time to stand, she dove off the patio and into the pool, leaving him with the vision of hips that his fingers itched to hold and an ass that he couldn't wait to see bent over the bed in front of him.

Victoria

O f all the times for a wardrobe malfunction, in the pool with Aaron was not ideal. Having purchased the bikini for her vacation but had never worn it in any body of water. She didn't think about the possibility of the cups coming down and exposing herself in front of a stranger when she surfaced after an easy dive.

"You all right?" he asked when she squeaked at the realization that her entire upper body was exposed as she surfaced, and if Aaron had been on the other side of her, he would have been treated to a free show.

Seeing him in his swim trunks without a shirt for the first time, she had been trying not to stare at the tattoos on his chest and dove in without giving any thought to her angle of entry into the water. As much as she enjoyed seeing him without his shirt on, she wasn't ready to exchange chest views with him quite yet, especially not outdoors where anyone could see them.

She fumbled with her top, trying to stuff herself back in before he realized what was happening and made the situation even more awkward. "I'm good," she said.

"Need any help there?" His voice sounded from directly behind her shoulder.

"What? Oh my god, I'm trying to get my top back on," she said, laughing, and hunching her shoulders to keep herself hidden.

"Like I said, need any help?"

When she had gotten herself together, she turned to see the wicked grin on Aaron's face and was struck again by how attractive he was. But it didn't change the fact that he was a musician, and she didn't date musicians. She took herself and her career far too seriously to spend her money supporting him or fighting a stereotype as some sex-crazed groupie willing to share her man with other women.

The reality of being forty-five made the likelihood of being looked at as a groupie virtually zero, but it didn't stop her brain from imagining it.

The back door opened, drawing their attention, and Hattie poked her head out. "Are you two planning to stay for dinner tonight? We're doing cold cut sandwiches with garden salad, pasta salad, and potato chips."

"I'm staying," Victoria said.

"If she stays, I stay," Aaron added.

She didn't know what to say to that or how to feel about his words. He was sending clear signals that he was interested in her and while she liked being near him, she just didn't know if it was something she could encourage. Could it simply be vacation sex like Paige had suggested? Was she built that way?

Would there be any harm in figuring it out as long as they both went their separate ways at the end of the week? She didn't have casual sex as a general rule, but even the on-again, off-again friends with benefits situations she had in the past were comfortable enough to not be awkward when they ended. Could she have casual sex with Aaron and then still see him around the inn for the rest of her time there?

A year was a very long time and she couldn't think of a better person to break her dry spell.

"Good enough," Hattie said. "Last night of just you two. Three more rooms reserved for tomorrow through the weekend. They're all coming in for a family wedding so it should be a little livelier around here going forward."

Though it was undoubtedly good for their business to keep a full inn, Victoria's heart squeezed at the realization that things had to change already. Knowing it was only herself and Aaron in the big old house had a sense of excitement. Hattie and Mitch had their own private residence off the side of the house, so in the guest rooms it was only her and Aaron.

A feeling of missed opportunity floated into her consciousness though she chose not to dwell on it because she still wasn't sure if she was going to act on any opportunity that may present itself.

Hattie looked from one of them to the other, her face quirked into a small smile, then she turned and disappeared into the house again, leaving Victoria to wonder if Hattie was up to something.

Victoria

S he planned Wednesday to be the highlight of her vacation. Before she'd left the city, Victoria had reserved a ticket to see the Boston Symphony Orchestra play at Tanglewood, the beautiful venue surrounded by nature in every direction, that was the Symphony's home every summer. She'd seen the BSO multiple times in Boston but found that she was looking forward to seeing them in the more relaxed, open space of Tanglewood.

"Are you sure you don't want to take a picnic basket?" Hattie asked as they enjoyed a cup of coffee together on the front porch, Hattie on the swing, Victoria on a small couch. Breakfast had been served and cleaned up, and the two women sat together before Hattie had to start getting rooms ready for their new arrivals.

"No, thank you," Victoria said. "I don't have lawn tickets, so I'm afraid I won't have anywhere to enjoy a picnic."

"Tickets for what?" Aaron's voice preceded him out the door and Hattie's smile once again had Victoria feeling like she was on the outside of a private joke.

"Miss Lathrop is going to the symphony tonight over at Tanglewood," Hattie answered for her.

"Is that so?" He held a cup of coffee in one hand and looked pointedly at the chair next to where Victoria sat. "May I?"

A thrill of anticipation fluttered in her belly. "Of course." She sipped her coffee. "Have you been to Tanglewood before?"

"Nope. I've been to a lot of venues but that's one I haven't seen."

"You should go with her," Hattie offered. "It's a great place to see a performance. It's super laid back and relaxed and the music is just wonderful." A dreamy look crossed her face as she clasped her hands and held them over her heart.

And there it was. Those little smirks and knowing looks. Hattie was one hundred percent playing matchmaker. Giving up any pretense, Hattie had just invited Aaron out on Victoria's behalf.

The expression on Aaron's face told her he'd been shocked when Hattie made her suggestion, but he didn't bother to gracefully decline either.

"As much as I'd like that, I only have the one ticket," Victoria said, then had second thoughts when she imagined Aaron dressed up and walking with her arm in arm. "Though, I suppose we could look and see if the one next to me is open."

"Sure," he said. "It's worth a shot."

Her arms grew heavy with disappointment when she looked at the venue's seating chart on her phone. Every seat in her section had been sold. "Sorry," she said. "Looks like nothing's open."

"Don't worry about it," he said, pulling up the site on his own phone. After a few clicks and swipes he said, "There. I just bought a lawn ticket." He looked at Hattie. "Any chance of getting a picnic basket for our evening out?"

Aaron

"It's not exactly the experience I had in mind when I bought my ticket," Victoria told him as she reached into the basket and pulled out the chocolate covered strawberries Hattie had packed for them. "And though it pains me to say it, I have to admit this might be better."

Her demeanor was soft and relaxed as they lounged on a blanket in the soft grass outside the music hall. "You didn't need to sit out here with me," he said. "I told you we could have eaten together and then you could go inside." He meant it yet was beyond thrilled that she chose to spend the evening with him outside on the lawn.

She rested back onto her splayed hands, tilted her head up toward the slowly darkening sky as it shaded from light blue to dark blue and into hints of violet. "But then I would have missed out on this." Looking over at him, she said, "Do you even know the last time I ate out of a picnic basket?" Her smile was radiant as she reached into the basket again and pulled out the stack of chocolate chip cookies Hattie threw in as extra dessert.

They shared the cookies as the music began, his eyes on Victoria more than anywhere else. He lived his whole life around music and as beautiful as it was, it only added to the overall feel of whatever was beginning between him and the lovely woman by his side.

Throughout the evening he would glance at her, with her eyes closed, lost in the music as her body swayed gently with the tempo of the piece. More than once he wished they were anywhere but in the middle of a crowded lawn so he could reach over and touch her, run his hand up her legs, over her belly and up to her breasts. He wanted to lean over and place a kiss on those sweet pink lips that were so quick to smile.

At that moment, her eyes popped open as if she'd been reading his mind, then she flashed him one of those smiles and returned her attention to the stage.

Once the performance ended and they were back in the car, he struck up a conversation as they waited in the line of traffic to exit the grounds. With any other person his question may have seemed abrupt, but something about Victoria told him she wouldn't mind. "How come you're out here on vacation by yourself?" he asked when the time seemed right.

She flicked a glance his way and said, "I'm afraid if I tell you, you'll think I'm weird."

He thought back on all the strange people he'd met over the course of the life of a successful musician and laughed. "I know weird. Trust me when I say you're not weird." She pulled the car up another couple lengths before she decided to answer him.

"Friday is my birthday and it's kind of a big one," she finally said. "Paige convinced me to come out here to celebrate while I stave off the breakdown she swears is brewing."

He'd only known Victoria a few days, but she already appeared less uptight than she did when she arrived on Monday. Sounded like her assistant knew what she was talking about.

"Is it working? Are you feeling less stressed out than when you got here?"

Without looking at him, she nodded her head. "You know, I think it is working. I haven't called the office once to check in, even though I really wanted to a few times." She sighed. "It's hard leaving your baby in someone else's hands, even if it's only for a week."

"That makes sense," he said. "But good for you for not calling. I assume they'd call you if something major was going down?"

"They would. So, I've just got to trust that I hired well and then trust them to do their jobs."

"Would you mind if I got nosy and asked which big birthday you're celebrating?" He laughed and threw in, "And, yes, my mother taught me you're never supposed to ask a woman her age. But I'm asking anyway."

Without a second's hesitation she said, "Forty-five."

Only two years younger than himself but she looked more like thirty-five than forty-five. "Can I press my luck and ask you something else I probably shouldn't?"

"Why am I spending my birthday by myself?" she offered.

"The thought had crossed my mind," he said. "Is there a Mr. Victoria at home?"

Laughing, she said, "Nope. No Mr. Victoria. I was married once years ago, but it didn't work out and I've been a little busy building a successful business from the ground up to have had time to find another one." Her tone was light, and he would have expected a hint of defensiveness but didn't hear any.

"You sound like you're all right with that."

As the train of cars neared the exit, she turned to face him. "Perfectly all right." Then she turned out of the lot and pulled onto the main road again. "Why wouldn't I be?"

She was beautiful, confident, and perfectly content to be on her own. So why did he suddenly want nothing more than to make her his?

Victoria

The ride back to the Faraway went by in a flash. The new people Hattie told them about had arrived and several of them had found the game room and, from the sound of it, were having a heated battle of eight ball.

Hattie and Mitch had turned in for the evening and Victoria was unexpectedly at a loss for words. She was walking on a cloud after her evening with Aaron and didn't want it to end. She struggled with the unfamiliar feeling of not knowing how to ask for what she wanted. Speaking up for herself and going after what she wanted was what Victoria had always been about. What was it about this man that had her completely out of sorts?

He seemed to be heading toward the stairs, so she did the same, as if it was her plan the whole time. Stopping to let her go before him, she reached the top first and waited for him to get there, her fingers suddenly jittery.

"Thanks for letting me crash your plans tonight." His voice was quiet as he leaned in and placed a kiss on her cheek. Then, much to her liking, he kissed her again. And again, getting slowly nearer to her mouth until she turned to meet his lips with her own.

"Thank you for coming with me," she said, leaning her forehead against his chest once the kiss had ended. "I had a lot of fun with you." She meant it. Even though she had a seat inside the hall quite near to the stage, sitting out on the lawn with Aaron had been like breathing extra oxygen; it left her lightheaded and giddy.

His fingertips found her cheek, brushed the hair back over her shoulder, then tilted her face toward his. He lowered his mouth to hers again, hungrier this time, but still soft enough to make her knees weak.

"Thanks for letting me invite myself," he said softly, then moved his hands from her face, lowered them to rest on her hips.

"I'm pretty sure Hattie invited you, but just the same, I'm glad you came with me." She laughed gently and Aaron began walking her backwards and kissing her again, deeper, letting his tongue dip into her mouth to dance with hers.

"Where are we going?" she whispered against his mouth.

"Your room? My room? Makes no difference to me." The words were barely out of his mouth before he crushed her with another kiss.

Rowdy voices from downstairs grew louder as the new guests began making their way toward their rooms.

She broke the kiss long enough to say, "My room?"

Then taking him by the hand she led the way around the banister and down the hall, slid the key into the lock. His body pressed against hers and she could feel by his hardness that he was just as ready as she was. But this wasn't a regular hotel. This was essentially a big house with random people staying in the various bedrooms. She had no idea how soundproof the walls or doors were.

As they stepped into the room, he spun her around and headed her toward the bed, kicking the door shut behind him.

"Can we do this in a bed and breakfast?" she asked, pressing her hands to his chest to hold him back for an extra second.

"That depends," he said, leaning in and kissing the side of her neck below her ear. "How quiet can you be?"

"Honestly? I don't know," she admitted, every part of her body on high alert. "I guess it depends on how good you are."

He chuckled low in his chest then pulled her in close, plunged his tongue into her mouth and kissed her until she needed to break free to catch her breath, her heart banging against the inside of her rib cage as her entire body flooded with heat.

The noise of voices in the hallway, doors opening and closing, all fell away as she pulled at Aaron's shirt, fumbled with his buttons until it was open enough to pull over his head. She'd seen his chest when they were in the pool but being close enough and now having the opportunity to touch him brought shivers to her belly that radiated into her trembling fingers.

Touching him, running her hands along his solid body, fueled the heat that burned through her. Suddenly she needed to see the rest of him, to see if the parts that had been covered by swim trunks were as impressive as the top half. Standing on tiptoes she leaned in to kiss him again as she worked the button and fly on his jeans. His hands threaded through her hair, and he leaned into the kiss as he let her undress him.

Pushing his pants down off his hips she slid her hand into the waistband of his boxers, wrapped her fingers around the biggest erection she'd ever felt. He groaned against her mouth as she began stroking him. "That's amazing," he whispered.

Encouraged by his words, she lowered her hand further until she reached his balls, let her fingers dance delicately for a few seconds before she gripped his shaft and stroked again. Aaron tilted his hips then rocked with the rhythm of her motion, whispering groans and grunts as she gripped a little tighter.

Precum slicked her fingers and with her free hand she pushed his boxers down, freeing him and giving her an incredible visual. Big and thick and hard in her hand, she involuntarily clenched thinking about him being inside of her when reality reared its ugly, albeit necessary, head. "Do you have a condom, by any chance?"

Between breaths he said, "Front pocket of my jeans."

Relief pumped through her veins. "Thank God," she said, then pushed his clothes entirely off his body, leaving him naked and hard and so hot.

Her tumbling thoughts clarified into a moment of doubt. "Wait," she said. "You knew we'd be sleeping together tonight? Am I that predictable?"

He laughed. "Not quite," he replied, as if he wasn't standing completely naked in front of her. "I figured the best-case scenario would be us having sex, which meant we'd need a condom. Worst case would be us wanting to have sex and neither of us having a condom. Either way, a condom was one hundred percent necessary."

Solid logic.

She reached out to take hold of him again, but he stilled her hand. "My turn," he said, then pushed her backward onto the bed. "This is the part where you need to remember to be quiet."

The word anticipation took on a whole new meaning as she watched Aaron climb onto the bed and kneel between her feet. His eyes raked over her body even though she was fully clothed. Taking hold of her hands, he pulled her up to sitting, then tugged her dress out from underneath her before yanking it clean over her head and tossing it to the floor. "Much better," he said. "Almost perfect." His eyes landed on her black lace bra. "That needs to come off."

She reached around and unclasped her bra, letting it fall away while Aaron sat, stroking himself as he watched. His eyes carved a path down her body and stopped at the scrap of black lace that served as underwear. "Now those." After wiggling her panties over her hips, exposing her bare skin to his gaze, Aaron's mouth pulled into a lopsided grin. "Now that's perfect."

Victoria leaned back onto her elbows as his fingers lightly grazed her skin, starting behind her knees and slowly inching up her thighs, toward her center. The heat that had been blazing in her veins was dangerously close to spontaneous combustion. Instinctively she pulled her knees closer together. "Nope," he said, pushing them back apart. "Those stay open, Victoria."

Her experience of him so far had been as an easy going, fun-loving guy. The bossy side she saw as he took control of the situation turned her on almost as much as seeing him naked and kneeling in front of her.

"You like being the boss of me right now?" she asked, though it was more statement than question.

His eyes ignited as he locked eyes with her, holding her motionless with his stare as his fingers glided up her thighs then slid inside of her. The urge to cry out, to moan, to whimper as he moved within her was overwhelming and she had to choke the noises down to keep the other guests from knowing what was currently happening in Room 4, top of the stairs, left around the banister, last door on the right.

"More to the point," Aaron said as she squirmed beneath his hands. "I know you like it when I'm the boss of you, don't you?"

Her yes came out as more of a strangled whimper which turned into a frustrated groan as he stilled his hands, his fingers still inside her.

"I'm going to make you come now, Victoria." He still hadn't moved his hand and she began to move her hips to force him to keep going.

"But you have to be a good girl and not be so loud the people around us know what I'm doing to you." Slowly, tortuously, his fingers moved and then he took them away. "Can you do that? Can you be quiet, so the neighbors don't hear when I make you come?"

A shiver of excitement tore through her body as he knelt in front of her, lowering his mouth, but stopping just shy of her skin. "I can't eat your pussy until you tell me you're going to be quiet." His warm breath danced over her already overheated skin.

"I'll try," she whispered, lifting her hips to press herself to his mouth.

He pulled his head away and held a hand on her belly. "Victoria," he said, voice full of warning, and she almost orgasmed without him even touching her.

"OK," she whispered. "I promise."

Her legs fell open and she watched as he slid his hands under her ass and pulled her against his mouth. His tongue swirled around her clit then he sucked gently as he dragged his hand from beneath her and slid two fingers inside. Unable to support herself on her elbows any longer, she dropped back onto the mattress and focused on feeling every point of contact between his mouth and fingers and her body.

Her breaths came in ragged gasps and turned toward whimpers as he licked her, flicking his tongue against her clit before sucking on it with a gentle pressure. He had clearly done this before, and she sent a silent thank you to whoever let him practice because she was sure this was the best oral sex ever given since the dawn. Of. Time.

Looking down her body again she watched his head move and she focused on the sounds, obscene to anyone overhearing, but pure bliss to her.

He lifted his face just long enough to say, "God, you taste so fucking good."

Her whimpers turned to outright groans and moans as he lowered his head again. Abruptly he stopped, looked up and caught her eye. "I'm not done with you yet. You need to be quiet."

"OK," she said, nodding, but desperate for him to keep going. "Please don't stop."

With a wicked grin he kissed her again, looked her in the eyes and said, "I'll keep going and make you come but if I have to tell you to be quiet again…" Without finishing the threat, he went back to trying to kill her with pleasure.

The tingling sensation started to build in her feet and in her fingers, rolling its way toward her core. Grabbing onto the sheets to keep from floating right off the bed, she pushed her hips into his face, matching the rhythm of his mouth and his fingers. Her gasps turned to whines and as the lightning rolled through her body, she couldn't control the shriek that escaped her lungs as she shook from the pure intensity of her orgasm.

Her panting breaths hadn't evened out yet when Aaron grabbed her legs, flipped her onto her belly and hiked her hips up and back. His big, warm body pressed against her ass as he leaned over her. "You screamed, Victoria." He leaned back then landed a gentle smack across her ass cheek. "You promised you were going to be a good girl and keep quiet. Now you're going to have to keep your face toward the mattress while I fuck you."

Every bone in her body dissolved at once listening to his words. Her ass still stung, and she pressed it back toward him anyway.

"Are you ready to be fucked until you scream again, Victoria?"

Every time he called her by name it sent a pang of need through her. Hearing her name from his mouth as he touched her, fingered her, even as he admonished her, turned her on in ways she'd never felt, not even with her ex-husband.

"God, yes," she whimpered and waited while he slid off the bed to grab the condom from his pants pocket. Then he was behind her again, the front of his thighs pressed against the back of hers. Looking over her shoulder she watched him stroke himself a few times with one hand before he rolled the condom on.

Aaron

Lining up behind her, he paused even as she pressed back against him, trying to push herself onto him. Having sex with this woman was everything he thought it would be, and then some. She was open and trusting and had a sense of fun that spoke to how good things could be between them if they only had more time together.

And suddenly that's what he wanted, more time. But with more time would come the necessity of letting her in and telling her who he was.

He closed his eyes and cleared his mind of any 'what comes next' thoughts, focusing solely on what was happening at that very moment. "Are you ready?" he said. "Because I need to be inside you now."

"Yes," she whispered. "Please."

Slowly he pressed the tip of his cock into her. He knew he was large and that he could cause pain if he wasn't careful. But the need to be buried inside Victoria's body almost made him forget that. He slid in a little further and she hissed as she clenched around him, turning her face into the mattress. Once she relaxed, he eased into her about halfway then waited for her to adjust. "You all right?" he asked.

"God, yes," she said.

Looking down at her ass, he rubbed his hands over her cheeks, pulled almost all the way out before squeezing his fingers into her hips for leverage and thrusting into her with a grunt.

Her gasp was muffled by the bedding, but he heard it and he needed to hear it again. Holding onto her hips, again and again he pulled out before slamming back in, their skin smacking together with each thrust. She lifted onto her forearms, and in the mirror, he watched her breasts bounce in rhythm as he fucked her. Turning her head, she locked eyes with his reflection.

The look of ecstasy on her face would be burned into his memory until the day he died. Her eyes fluttered closed seemingly against their will every time he buried himself, her bottom lip pulled up and held between her teeth.

He needed to come but he wanted her to come again before he finished. "I'm going to make you scream into the mattress now," he said as he stilled his hips, reached his arms forward to play with her breasts. Her nipples were hard against his fingertips, and she clenched around his cock every time he pinched them. "Are you ready to come again for me, Victoria?"

Without waiting for an answer, he pulled back and drove into her, hard. She dropped her head to the mattress as she cried out. "Clench your pussy around me," he said, and she did. So slowly it just about killed him, he pulled all the way out against the pressure of her muscles. Dipping his finger between her lips, he touched her clit and rubbed small circles around it, lubricating his fingers with her arousal.

He could have spent the entire night enjoying her pussy, eating it, fingering it, fucking it.

"Please, Aaron," she whined.

"Please, what, Victoria?"

"Please make me come. Please."

Moving his fingers from her clit, he slid them back to her entrance and fucked her with his fingers. "Is that what you want? Is that how you like it?"

"Please," she begged. "I need you to fuck me now."

Replacing his fingers with his cock, Aaron rocked into her, her sighs of contentment his reward. So far, she'd been willing to go along with his take charge game, and he wondered how far he could push her. As he pounded into her, he brought one hand to her ass, brushed a finger against the tight hole.

"Oh, my god," she cried out.

He pressed the tip of his finger inside and he thought she might implode if her panting and whimpering meant anything. A few seconds later, with no real warning, Victoria screamed into the bed as her entire body trembled against his, giving him the permission he needed to let go. He rutted into her with a growl, his body eventually stilling, before he pulled out and she collapsed beneath him into a boneless, giggling heap.

Victoria

Aaron had gone into the bathroom to clean up while Victoria threw on a bathrobe and flopped back down onto the bed, completely relaxed and exhausted.

"So," he said, coming back into the bedroom, picking up his clothes from the heap on the floor. He pulled his shirt over his head. "I hope this isn't where the awkwardness starts."

She threw her head back and laughed. "This? You think this is where it would get awkward?" Coming back up to sitting, she let her leg hang over the edge of the bed. "What just happened here—" she swirled her arms around in a circle over the bed. "If *that* wasn't awkward, then this part should be a breeze."

His easy smile warmed her, and she realized he wasn't feeling the least bit weird around her, but was, in fact, making sure she was OK with what they just did. Not surprisingly, she was entirely OK with it. She had enjoyed it from beginning to end and wondered how soon they'd be able to do it again.

After he finished pulling on his pants he sat on the other side of the bed from her, leaned over and said, "Well, if you're good, I'm good."

"I'm good," she said. "I am most definitely good."

He glanced over his shoulder, looked her up and down. "Yeah," he said. "You are."

Even pushing forty-five years old wasn't enough to keep the blush from burning into her cheeks at his compliment. "How exactly does this work now?" she asked.

"How do you mean?"

"Not that I have random sex with strangers all that often," she teased. "But normally they leave, and we go on with our lives. But you're literally staying in the room across the hall. How am I supposed to avoid you if it's uncomfortable tomorrow when we see each other?"

Aaron chuckled, grabbed her hand, and gave a gentle squeeze. "For the record, I'm also not a sex with strangers kind of person. But since you brought it up, how about we don't get uncomfortable when we see each other tomorrow? That sounds like the easiest solution to me."

It sounded like an easy solution in theory, but could she do it in practice? She'd had a few somewhat steady boyfriends over the past few years, on and off again, regular, safe guys that she enjoyed spending time with. But none of them ever held her interest in the way that Aaron Price already did. The little bit of time they spent together was some of the most enjoyable time she'd had in recent memory. He was easy to talk with and he was fun to be around. The sex was, without exaggeration, the best she'd ever had, and it was only their first time.

"You know I'm leaving at the end of the week, right?" she said. "Even if we aren't uncomfortable tomorrow, we only have a few days left of this." Her heart took on an unexpected heaviness as the words left her mouth. She didn't want their time together to be ending when it was only just getting started, even though she knew there was no chance of any kind of future between them.

He leaned toward her again, pressed a kiss onto her cheek. "Then let's enjoy the few days we have together." When he stood to leave, she wanted to reach out her hand and pull him back down onto the bed to stay with her. But inviting him to spend the night in her room might be a bit too much a bit too fast. She watched as he slowly opened the door and poked his head into the hallway. Pulling it back in, he said with a laugh, "Coast is clear. Looks like all our housemates have turned in for the night."

"Oh good." She started giggling at the absurdity of the whole situation. He turned to see what she was laughing at. "Sorry," she said. "It's just that watching you be afraid to leave my room because you might get caught has a very comedy movie vibe to it, like as soon as you step through the door my dad's going to come walking around the corner and kick your ass down the stairs and out the door."

To her surprise he returned to where she sat on the bed, leaned down and kissed her one more time before he pulled away from her. "It still would have been worth it," he said.

Victoria did her best thinking while she relaxed in the tub, so once the door clicked closed behind him, she turned the lock then went to the big claw foot tub. She opened the taps and let the tub fill so she could sit and soak while she figured out what to do about her Aaron Price problem.

Aaron

By the time he finished his second cup of coffee, Aaron had given up waiting for Victoria. He had a busy day ahead of him and Alyssa was scheduled to arrive sometime in the next hour so they could talk more seriously about the nuts and bolts of running a business like the Faraway Inn. They had a meeting scheduled with Hattie and Mitch for lunch which included a more formal tour of the building as well as a discussion of the inner workings of running the inn.

The time available to see Victoria dwindled by the second. Breakfast had barely settled, and he already knew lunch and dinner with her were both out of the question. Aside from the meeting with the innkeepers, he and Alyssa already had plans to eat dinner at a pub in town. Bringing Victoria along didn't seem fair to Alyssa or entirely comfortable for Victoria.

As if thinking about her brought her into existence, she appeared beside him like a vision from a dream. "Hey, sleepy head," he said. "I was beginning to wonder if maybe you'd already taken off for the day and I missed you."

"Nope," she said as she settled onto the sofa next to him. "I completely overslept. I haven't needed an alarm in close to a decade and today I slept later than I have in all that time." Her smile was so relaxed and sweet he had no choice but to smile back. Taking a sip of the coffee clutched in her hand, she said, "It was such a restful sleep, I almost didn't want to get out of bed."

"Oh yeah, why did you then?" he asked, hoping she would tell him how much she couldn't wait to see him, seeing as how she was the first thing on his mind as soon as he opened his eyes that morning.

With both hands she raised her mug to her lips, inhaled the steam wafting off the top. "Coffee." She grinned and took a sip.

Victoria

O nce he stopped laughing, his face turned serious, apologetic before he said, "I hope you don't take this the wrong way, but I'm not going to be able to spend any time with you today. My daughter's supposed to be getting here in a little while and we have a ton of stuff to do and see with Hattie and Mitch."

She knew the whole reason for him being at the Faraway was because he was doing research on whether it would be a good investment for his daughter, but she couldn't ignore the pinch in her chest when he told her they couldn't see each other during the day. Of all people, she knew how important work was and there weren't many people who could drag her away from her own. Still, the sting of disappointment was real.

"Totally fine," she said, though she only half meant it. "How about dinner?"

He frowned as he crossed his arms over his chest, and she knew dinner was out of the question too. "Sorry," he said. "I already promised Alyssa I'd take her out tonight. But she's got some more work to do with Hattie and Mitch, so I'll be available tomorrow if you're still up for hanging around with me."

Friday was her birthday, and she had originally planned to take a mixology class at a local restaurant, Eddie's on the Green, by herself to celebrate. The registration fee even included her own cocktail making set to take home. When she had called to see if she could bring a plus-one, she ended up canceling because the class was already full. She hadn't even asked Aaron to know if he was interested or available, she just knew she didn't want to go alone anymore.

"I was planning to lay out and then do a little swimming tomorrow," she said. "But you're welcome to join me."

"You going to wear that black two piece again?"

Heat flamed through her, and she nodded. "It's the only suit I brought with me, so, yeah."

At that moment, Aaron was a study in desire; lips parted, eyes roaming her body, chest lifting and lowering on deepening breaths. Crossing her arms over her body, she curled back into the couch, remembering the same way he looked at her the night before and liking it just as much as she did then.

"Then I'll be there," he said, letting his fingers graze her thigh. "It's going to be hard waiting to see you until tomorrow."

The front door to the inn opened and a young woman dressed in white pants and a sleeveless purple top stepped through, dropped her travel bag to the floor and said, "Hey, Dad." The woman's eyes darted between Victoria and Aaron.

He hopped up from the couch and wrapped his daughter in a big hug. "Hey, Sweetheart, how was the trip? Didn't take you as long as you thought it would?"

Alyssa's eyes flicked over to Victoria then back to her father. "Yeah, there wasn't any traffic so I'm a little earlier than I thought."

Victoria knew it was time to get dressed and let Aaron and his daughter get on with their day. While he was busy with Alyssa, she spent the morning by the pool, a book from the game room in one hand and a tall glass of lemonade in the other. As much as she tried to focus on the words on the pages, her mind wandered back to her dates with Aaron. The sex was incredible, but it was the conversation over dinner, over chocolate, on the lawn outside the music hall that kept drawing her memory.

She needed to occupy herself making new memories, new things to tell Paige and her other friends when she returned to Boston. To keep herself from getting too attached to her handsome new friend, after a quick shower, she dressed, threw her hair in a ponytail, and got ready for her collage class at the art center in Stockbridge, about forty miles away.

Several hours later, her collage laid out and drying in the trunk of her car, she sat in a small diner about halfway between Stockbridge and Hazelton, eating a Caesar salad and bowl of chicken noodle soup when a text came through from Paige.

> *Everything OK? Haven't heard from you in a couple days??*

Victoria smiled as she responded.

> *Everything is fine. Having a great time.*

> *Yay!!! So you had sex with him?*

> *WTH??*

> You haven't contacted me since Monday.
>
> Today is Thursday.
>
> Not like you AT ALL.
>
> Which means you are busy doing something else...
>
> Namely the guy who liked your boobs.

She followed it up with the smirking face emoji and Victoria laughed at her inability to hide anything from her friend.

> Not having this convo thru text.
>
> I knew I was right!!!
>
> Was it awesome?

Victoria responded with a smiling face emoji and put her phone back into her purse while she finished her lunch, ignoring the ringing of Paige calling for details. She couldn't have stopped smiling if she tried to.

Aaron

The entire point of coming to the Faraway was to help Alyssa learn about and gain a deeper understanding of how hard it would be run a business like this, yet throughout the day Aaron's mind drifted back to Victoria. During lunch with Alyssa, Hattie, and Mitch, he found himself wondering how her class went and how soon she'd be back. Though it didn't matter because he didn't have any free time to spend with her. Out of nowhere his jaw clenched as he wondered if she met any new guys while she was out without him.

Of course, that would be none of his business, but he couldn't help but wonder. Why did that bother him as much as it did? Jealousy wasn't normally his way of operating, but he had no idea where things stood with Victoria or how serious she wanted to get with him, when the more he thought about her, the more he wanted to know her and spend time with her.

Life as a rock star, as much as he hated that term, meant people always wanted to be around him and went out of their way to spend time with him. Victoria was different. She still gave no indication that she knew he was, and she seemed happy enough to spend time with him but was obviously just fine spending her time by herself.

"Everything OK, Dad?" Alyssa asked when Aaron appeared to ignore Mitch's questions for the third time in less than an hour. "You seem seriously preoccupied."

All eyes were on him as they waited for his response; Alyssa's brows pinched in confusion; Mitch's face was open with concern. Only Hattie wore a smile that told him she knew exactly where his mind was.

Ignoring Hattie, he turned to his daughter. "Sorry, Sweetheart. I guess I was a little distracted. But I'm fine now." He turned to Mitch. "What was it you were asking?"

Mitch scratched his head, started to laugh. "Honestly, I have no idea."

"Oh, Mitch," Hattie said. "If your head wasn't attached to your body..." She smiled affectionately at her husband and laid a hand on his arm. To Alyssa she said, "And that's why we're looking to sell the Faraway. It's time for us to leave all this hard work to the next generation."

Alyssa gave Aaron a pleading look. Even after everything they learned spending the day with Hattie and Mitch, how much work was involved in the day to day running of the inn, she still looked like she wanted to buy it. He couldn't discuss anything with her in front of the innkeepers, but they would certainly have a lot to talk about over dinner.

It had been a long day, bellies were grumbling all around, and then Hattie and Mitch had to get dinner prepared for their guests while Aaron and Alyssa went out to grab dinner in town. He shook Mitch's hand, then Hattie's, thanked them for the time they spent with him and Alyssa. "I think you have definitely given us a lot to think about and to discuss, right, Lyss?"

Alyssa nodded. "Definitely." Her smile stretched from one ear to the other and Aaron thanked rock and roll heaven for the incredible success he'd had to be able to afford to help his only child in pursuit of such a big dream. He had no idea if she'd be successful at it, but her nature was nothing short of tenacious when she had a goal in mind. And the Faraway was the biggest goal on which she'd ever set her sights.

By the time they left for dinner, he still hadn't seen Victoria come back to the inn. It was strange that he worried about her when he'd known her less than a week. Still, he couldn't hold back the smile when her Mercedes pulled into the driveway right as he closed the car door behind Alyssa. He waited the few extra seconds for Victoria to get out of her car before he walked over to his own door.

"Hey," he said as she caught his eye. "How was your class?"

"Surprisingly good," she said. "I'm leaving my collage in the trunk to dry."

He looked at the shopping bag in her hands. "You ended up at The Rockwell Museum? That's a great place. I checked it out on day two."

She glanced at his car, but his windows were tinted and there was no way she could see Alyssa sitting in the passenger's seat. "I had some time to kill, and I love his work," she said. "How did you guys do with Hattie and Mitch? Have you come to any decision about whether you're going to buy the place?"

The memory of Victoria on her bed, naked and open for him swam to the surface of his brain and he had to shuffle his feet to re-engage his brain for conversation. "No," he said. "No decisions yet. We're on our way out for dinner right now to talk things over and see what she's thinking." He shrugged, even though he had a fairly good sense of which way Alyssa would go.

"Don't let me keep you then," she said. "And if you're still planning to be around tomorrow, I'd love to hear how it all worked out." With a gentle smile she readjusted her grip on her shopping bag and walked into the inn, looking back quickly before she closed the door.

"OK, spill it," Alyssa said when he got into the car. "Who is she?"

"Just another guest who's been staying here this week. She's a nice person, though."

Alyssa laughed. "Oh, my God, Dad. Knock it off." She pushed his arm. "You like her." she said in a sing-song voice.

He did like Victoria, but it wasn't a topic he needed or wanted to talk about with Alyssa. "Like I said, she's a nice person. She and I went to Tanglewood yesterday." He pulled the car out of the driveway and headed it toward town.

Alyssa's eyes were fixed on him as he drove. "You went to see a concert with a complete stranger?"

He glanced at her then back at the road. "That's how dates work, so... yeah."

"Ooh," she squealed. "A date? It looked like you wanted to ask her for a second one. And it looked like she wanted you to ask her for a second one. Are you going to ask her out again?"

Aaron chuckled. He should have known better than to try and ignore the topic of his love life once Alyssa saw them together. He and Alyssa's mother had never officially been married but he still supported her financially until Alyssa turned twenty-one. After being together for a few years, their split wasn't entirely amicable; she was desperate to live up the life of rock stardom while he valued his privacy and needed his downtime. She ended up dating one musician after another while he endured the chaos of traveling the world to earn his living.

"Tomorrow is her birthday, so I was planning to take her out to celebrate," he said.

Alyssa clapped her hands. "Dad, that's awesome!"

"I guess. She's only here until Sunday so I don't know how awesome it is." The thought of her leaving tugged his heart, but he and Alyssa still had a lot to talk about that had nothing to do with Victoria. He pulled into the parking space in front of the restaurant. "Alright, kiddo. Enough about my love life. Let's go talk about the Faraway and what kind of plans you have for it."

Victoria

F riday morning dawned with Victoria sitting on the front porch swing, a cup of coffee in one hand and her journal closed in her lap. She was only a day older than she was yesterday but somehow officially turning forty-five felt like a Rubicon she'd crossed into another part of her life. Now when she thought about her age, she was closer to fifty than forty.

Her business was a resounding success; happy employees, happy clients, and a decent income made it hard to argue. Her apartment, decorated in modern shades and styles was one most people would be envious of. She leased a new luxury car every few years. By all accounts, she was every bit the success story her mother had raised her to be.

But as the sun continued its ascension on the first day of the next chapter of her life, she couldn't help but feel like something was missing. Her sister always told her she'd regret not having kids, that being the fun aunt would eventually get old. But that wasn't it. She wasn't suddenly pining to be a mother. Auntie Vic was a title she wore proudly, and she still had no interest in kids of her own.

Going back to her first love of art over the past week was supposed to help fill that empty space she had inside. And while she enjoyed herself immensely the past few days, the emptiness had only grown deeper. The love of creating art had never truly left her so finding it again brought a sense of peace, but she was beginning to wonder if sleeping with Aaron might not have been the best idea. It seemed that the emptiness wasn't as easily filled with other things since their hot as hell encounter.

The pinprick of that missing piece stabbed at her until she heard the front door open.

Wearing a dark gray t-shirt and a pair of faded jeans, with a chestnut brown acoustic guitar across his body, Aaron walked out to the porch and put his coffee on the railing. "Good morning," he said as he pulled over one of the chairs and sat near her.

"Morning," she said, suddenly lighter, as if she could float up and out of the swing. "Are you going to play for me?"

After he adjusted the guitar on his leg, he winked at her and began to strum. Then, in the clearest, most beautiful voice she'd ever heard, Aaron sang her the birthday song while she sat on the swing and melted into a puddle. Her belly fluttered and her heart was full to bursting with so many feelings; surprise, gratitude, joy. Clasping her hands over her smiling mouth, she watched and listened as he sang only for her.

His body was relaxed, his eyes almost closed and when he finished singing, he sat with his arm draped over the body of the guitar. "Happy birthday, Victoria."

Her throat was thick with emotion, but she managed to squeak out two words. "Thank you."

After taking a quick sip of his coffee, he said, "But I'm not done yet." Resting his guitar against the railing, he disappeared into the inn only to come back a few seconds later holding a plate of chocolate covered strawberries piled around a muffin with a single lit candle stuck in the middle of it.

"For me?" she said, as he handed her the plate.

"Of course. You're the only person I know celebrating a birthday today." As she took the plate from his hand, he leaned down and placed a kiss on her cheek. Closing her eyes, she breathed him in, letting his clean scent wash over her, the desire for him completely overwhelming.

Scooting over, she made room for him on the swing.

He pulled out a pack of matches and lit the candle. "Make a wish."

It didn't take long to think of something to wish for. She closed her eyes. *Tell me what that missing piece is*, she wished, and hoped the universe understood her request as she blew out the candle.

When she opened her eyes, Aaron was looking at her and she wished she knew what he was thinking. His hands curled on his legs, and he opened his mouth as if he had something to say, then shook his head quickly and pressed his lips together.

"What?" Victoria said. "Did you want to say something?"

"Nope. Only wondering what you wished for," he said as she took a strawberry and bit into it, savoring the sweetness of the berry mixed with the dark chocolate coating.

Obviously, there was something else he wanted to say but it was up to him to say it. "Can't tell," she said. "You should already know that. If you tell someone your wish it won't come true."

He held her with a steady gaze that made her shift in her seat. "If you say so," he said then nodded at her coffee cup. "May I?" he asked. "Mine's all the way over there."

She handed him her coffee and was mildly surprised that she liked seeing him take a sip like they were old friends who did those kinds of things every day. Like it was completely normal.

"Extra sugar?" he asked, his face grimacing as handing back her cup. "You think you're not sweet enough already?"

Victoria laughed out loud and then groaned. "Seriously? What are you, in fourth grade? What kind of cheesy line was that?" His smile told her he was being intentionally ridiculous, and she liked how he looked at her. It hit her in all the same warm places his singing voice did. "You have a beautiful voice, by the way," she added. "I don't think I've ever had anyone sing me that song even remotely in tune before. Were you ever in a band or anything?"

Looking away from her, he cleared his throat. "I was in a band for a few years. No big deal." With twitchy fingers he picked up a strawberry and bit into it. "Aren't you going to eat your birthday muffin? Hattie made it special last night and left it in the refrigerator for me. She'd be heartbroken if you didn't eat it, you know."

There was more to Aaron Price than he was willing to share with her at present and she had no idea why. His demeanor in the bedroom the other night was almost entirely opposite the nervous mood he was obviously in. Since she'd most likely never see him again after the weekend she didn't ask.

"Pushy, pushy," she teased as she picked up the muffin and tore away the paper wrapper. Breaking the treat in half she handed one piece to him and held onto the other. "Here, you get half for singing to me."

"You said today was a milestone birthday," he said around his bite of chocolate chip muffin. "How's that going for you?"

She wasn't sure how to answer him, whether she should tell him the truth or keep things close to the vest, the same way he was obviously doing with her. "It's not bad so far," she answered, deciding on a combination of the two. "After lunch I still plan to go swimming if you're up for it."

"I'm most definitely up for it," he said, his tone lightening. "And if you're up for it, I would love to take you out for dinner tonight to keep the celebration going. There is a little brew pub on the edge of town that has live music and some lawn games and things like that I'd love to take you to."

"Games, huh?" she said with a mouthful of strawberry. "What are we betting on tonight?"

Watching him school his face into a neutral expression was hilarious. She hadn't meant it to be a sexual innuendo, but after it came out of her mouth there was no other way he could have interpreted it. She leaned into the naughtiness. "We deciding on who buys the first round?" she said. "Or are we talking sexual favors here? Either way is fine with me."

Her breathing was calm, though she couldn't help but smile at the fluttering butterflies of anticipation as she showered and dressed for her birthday evening out with Aaron.

Earlier in the afternoon she had set aside a couple hours to respond to birthday texts and to return her mother's phone call. While she told her mother she was having a wonderful time on her solo vacation, she neglected to mention the time she'd spent with Aaron.

Before that, they'd spent an hour in the pool and Aaron had told her all about his conversation with Alyssa, and how she surprised him by saying she needed a little more time to decide whether she wanted to buy the inn. They had a lot of numbers to look at and work with, and she wanted to talk to an accountant first.

But as she clasped her necklace and dabbed a few drops of perfume behind her ears, between her breasts, and behind her knees, her focus was solely on Aaron and wondering where the night would lead.

Of course, she hoped it would lead to sex, but with his daughter now staying at the inn, she had no idea how, or if, that would even be a possibility. She didn't even know which room Alyssa was staying in and that could be a disaster if they were too loud.

Was it just the relaxation of her vacation time or was there truly something happening between her and Aaron? She liked being around him. He made her laugh, and she loved how calm and casual he was, to say nothing about how hot he was, or how that calm and casual nature took a backseat to a take charge nature in bed. A tiny piece of her wondered if she only liked him so much because she knew her mother wouldn't. Was it some sort of teenage rebellion more than twenty-five years too late?

She didn't know all that much about him, only that he was a gifted musician, and he had a small apartment in New York City and a larger home with a bunch of land somewhere in upstate New York. He didn't talk much about himself or his career, only that he did a lot of traveling as a young man and needed a place to lay down roots. The beauty and solitude of his upstate home gave him a place to do that while being close enough to the city to maintain a presence in the world of music.

After hearing him sing even something as simple as the birthday song, Victoria didn't doubt that he belonged in that world. Thinking back to the deep, rich tones as he sang to her that morning lit a flame that filled her from head to toe, lingering at all the good parts in between.

A soft knock alerted her that he was outside her door. "Victoria?"

She twirled in front of the mirror to double check that her outfit looked as good as she hoped it did. It was a simple sundress, but the deep yellow color always made her feel pretty.

"Wow," he said, his mouth falling open, as she pulled the door open. "You look stunning."

Eyeing him quickly from top to bottom, she liked how he looked too; dark jeans and a teal Henley had never been so appealing to her. "Thank you," she said. "You look rather fabulous yourself."

He smiled at her compliment and held out his hand. "Shall we?"

Taking hold of his hand, she followed him out the door. "We shall."

He told her he was taking her to a local brewery, and she had imagined a small industrial building with a few tables scattered around a bar. To her surprise the brewery turned out to be an old, converted barn with a huge outdoor seating area. From the Mountain Tap Brewery's gravel parking lot, she saw a sprawling green lawn dotted with picnic tables, and clusters of Adirondack chairs around stone fire tables. It appeared the restaurant had a decent reputation for good food to go along with its great atmosphere. Couples and groups of people were enjoying themselves everywhere she looked.

The hostess grabbed their menus and led Victoria and Aaron out to the yard where they picked an open group of chairs around an unlit fire table. "Jesse will be right back to grab your drink order," the hostess said before she left the table.

"I hope this is all right for a celebratory dinner. I never did ask if you drink beer, but this place looked like so much fun I thought I'd take the chance," Aaron said as they settled into their chairs.

Victoria flipped her menu over to check out the dessert side then she looked around at all the people in the yard. A group of friends had gone over to play a game of corn hole, laughing riotously as one young man missed getting every bean bag through the hole on the wooden board. "I have to say I kind of love this place already," she said, turning her attention back to Aaron. "It has such a great vibe."

"And they have corn hole," he said.

"They do."

"Wanna play a game?" he asked.

"What are the stakes? I checked out the dessert menu and they have pecan pie, so we could always bet on who pays for that."

"We could," he said slowly. "But since I'm treating you to dinner and dessert for your birthday—"

She knew he was going to mention the whole sexual favor suggestion from earlier, but just as he was about to say it, a tall, college-aged young man approached the table. "Hey," he said in a voice so deep she almost didn't believe it came from someone so young. "I'm Jesse and I'll be taking care of you tonight. Can I start you off with our summer ale, or a New England IPA?"

Aaron looked to her to choose her drink before he ordered a tall IPA. "Would you like a basket of chips and salsa or anything else while we look at the menu?" Aaron asked her.

"Sure," she said. "Chips and salsa sound great."

Once Jesse left the table, Aaron looked back at her, leaned forward, and said, "So... about that bet." She was happy to be sitting down at that moment because had she been standing, her knees would have buckled at that grin on his face.

The summer sky had begun to darken, and the humidity rolled in along with the heavy clouds, hinting at the possibility of a thunderstorm. Aaron's evident desire for her only added to the heat that already surrounded them.

Looking around she saw that there was a corn hole game open a few feet from their table. "Boards are open if you want to play," she said and stood to grab a set of beanbags. She knew exactly what she was playing for.

As she stooped to pick up the set of orange beanbags, she felt his presence beside her and she looked up the length of him, lingering between his legs, as she thought back to the other night, then rose to face him. "You ready to lose this time, Price?"

Leaning in close and pressing a kiss to her cheek, he said, "Miss Lathrop, I am ready for anything life sends my way," then he turned and walked to take his place at the board opposite hers.

What the hell did that mean? It was Victoria's turn to stand with her mouth hanging open as she thought about his words. She closed her mouth just as he looked at the beanbags in her hand. "Ladies first."

Thunder rumbled in the distance as, with shaky hands, Victoria lined up to take her first shot, tossed it in a high arc, and watched it land on the board's surface. "One point for me," she said and grinned, confident that corn hole would be her game.

After she had tossed all four beanbags, her score totaled two, since one bag sailed right over the top of the board and the other landed on the edge then fell onto the grass. Her confidence in her skill faltered as Aaron stood, one leg behind the other and tossed one beanbag after the other toward the board by her feet. The first one missed entirely, but the second one dropped through the hole like it had found its forever home and couldn't wait to get there. The third and fourth landed flat on top of the board and his five points canceled out her two, leaving him up by three.

Lightning flashed over the mountains to the east, and a peal of thunder sounded after she finished counting to ten-Mississippi. The storm was far off but she didn't know if it was moving toward or away from Hazelton. Their server returned and dropped off their drinks so Victoria and Aaron returned to the table to place their dinner orders.

"Keep playing while we wait? I've only gotten to three, and I need a few more to win," he teased.

"You can go take some practice shots. I'll just wait here and eat some chips and salsa." She leaned back in her Adirondack chair, crossed one leg over the other and sipped her summer ale.

He stood behind her, ran his warm hands across her shoulders and squeezed them before he squatted behind her chair. "Why are you afraid to lose? We haven't even decided what we're betting on." His voice was as smooth as the dark chocolate they had for dessert the first night they went out together, bringing goose bumps to her entire body.

He returned to his seat, and they sat together eating chips and salsa in a highly charged silence until Jesse returned to drop off their dinners, all the while the lightning flashes growing brighter in a darkening sky, and the number of Mississippis before the thunderclaps dropped to two.

"Be ready to grab those and run to the barn," Aaron said, indicating her dinner and her beer. "That sky is looking meaner by the second."

She glanced around and noticed people bringing their dinners and their belongings into the big wooden barn and realized that was going to be them in about one minute. A crack of lightning bit the air, followed immediately by a clap of thunder so loud her body vibrated with the sound. She and Aaron snatched up their dinners and followed the group into the crowded barn as the sky opened up and the deluge of rain poured down.

They were able to snag a small high-top table in the middle of the room as the once empty space filled with people all hustling in out of the rain. "I'll be right back," Aaron said as he excused himself from the table.

Victoria continued to eat her veggie burger and fries while she waited for him, eventually thinking there must have been a long line at the men's room. *Now he knows how women always feel*, she thought with no sympathy at all. When she turned to look for him, she saw him talking with a group of people, all laughing and smiling and chatting as if they'd known each other for ages. One young man even threw an arm around Aaron's shoulder and snapped a quick selfie. After he shook the man's hand, Aaron pointed toward Victoria and departed his group of friends with a wave.

Looking from Aaron toward the crowd and back, she said, "What was that about?"

"Oh, just talking with a couple people. It's crowded in here and we got chatting as I walked by the bar. You know how it is." Whatever it was she had witnessed, Aaron clearly wanted to avoid talking about. "Can I get you another drink or anything?" he asked.

"No," she said. "I'm good with this one, thank you."

They finished their dinners and paid their bill when she noticed the air hockey table was, surprisingly, empty. "What do you think?" she said as they walked past it. "Finish our bet over there?"

A grin flashed across his face. "Absolutely."

Pool and corn hole may not have been her games, but youthful summers spent at Hampton Beach on the tiny piece of New Hampshire coastline meant lots of time at the boardwalk arcades, including hours of playing her favorite game, air hockey.

As the cool air blew up through the tiny holes on the tabletop, Victoria placed the flat plastic puck and readied herself to blow Aaron Price out of the water. With a quick snap of her wrist the puck flew down to his end, bounced around the corner and ricocheted into the goal in front of him.

Aaron's mouth fell open. "Whoa, what was that?" he asked with a laugh.

"That was you getting warmed up to lose, that's what that was." She leaned over the table and wiggled her hips getting ready for his return shot.

His eyes locked onto her breasts before he raised them to meet her eyes. "Pretty sure I can't lose here, even if you do score more points than me." His lips quirked up into a grin as he retrieved the puck and placed it onto the table.

There was a five-minute timer on the game, but Victoria only needed two of those minutes to rack up a score of four to one. By the time the air shut off, she had increased her lead to seven to two, securing her first victory against Aaron.

Planting her feet, she squared her shoulders. "Play again?" she asked.

Aaron

The rain pounded the roof overhead, and the noise of the crowd grew as people had to shout to be heard. A few groups of guys hung around the air hockey table. He figured partly they were waiting for him and Victoria to leave so they could take over the game, and partly they were enjoying the show when she leaned over the table. He couldn't blame them, but he also had no intention of letting it continue.

Luckily, they weren't the same guys who had noticed him on his way out of the men's room earlier. He hardly ever minded when people recognized him, but he hadn't planned on coming clean with Victoria in the middle of a crowded restaurant. Eventually he had to tell her, especially since he planned on continuing things with her after her vacation ended, but he was enjoying the way she looked at him, simply as he was, not as some larger than life rock star.

She hadn't pushed him on why some random guy took a selfie with him at the bar, but he knew, eventually, it was coming.

"I was thinking of taking you over to the little coffee shop in town to grab some dessert. We'll give some of these other people a chance to play," he said.

With a shrug she said, "It's cool if you just can't handle getting your ass kicked by a girl. I get it." The grin on her face pulled at every piece of his heart. He loved playing against her, win or lose, because she threw her whole self into everything she did and enjoyed the competition as much as he enjoyed her company.

"Something like that," he said and led her through the crowd with his hand on her back, his possessiveness suddenly very real. "Why don't you wait here, and I'll go bring the car up to get you."

She tugged him to a stop. "I'm not made of sugar, I won't melt. Come on." Then she pulled him along into the downpour as they ran together toward his car. He attempted to open the passenger door for her, but she shocked him by pushing it closed with her hip then flinging her arms around his neck, hauling him down for a kiss in the rain.

The rain drenched his face, his back, his arms, but all he felt was Victoria's soft body against his, her tongue dancing with his own, her fingers lacing through his hair.

Finally, she released him, blinking rain drops out of her eyelashes. "Sorry," she said. "Couldn't help myself." Grinning up sheepishly at him she said, "I didn't even think about how wet your seats are going to be now."

"Don't worry about it. They'll dry," he said as he opened the door for her, then hurried over to his side, his tongue darting out to lick his lip where her lips had just been.

As they drove away from the restaurant, the rain kicked into gear again, making it difficult to see where he was going. Even with his windshield wipers furiously working to clear the glass, he knew they were outmatched my Mother Nature, so he pulled the car off to the side of the road to wait it out until the heaviest rain passed by.

He was about to strike up another conversation when she shocked him for the second time by opening her door, and slamming it shut before she whipped open the back door and jumped into the back seat with a whoosh. "What are you doing?" he asked, turning to face her.

With her feet on either side of the bump in the back seat, she sat with her dress scrunched up in her hands, her shoulders back. "Waiting for you," she said.

Not one to miss an opportunity like that, he climbed over the center console and tumbled into the seat beside her. Before he could speak, she had thrown one leg over his lap and straddled him, her barely covered breasts impossibly close to his mouth. Her lips were on his in an instant, and just as instant was the erection he pressed into her center as she ground herself against him.

The chemistry between them crackled with as much intensity as the storm that raged around them as hands roamed, groped, caressed, and teased. "You sure you want to do this in a car?" he asked in between kissing her mouth and kissing the tops of her breasts. "It's not like we're kids who have nowhere else to have sex."

"I guess I should have told you," she said. "This is what I won when I beat you at air hockey."

He pulled himself away, unable to stop the laugh that bubbled up. "What?"

"I was betting against myself, and if I lost, I promised I would leave you be, but if I won, I was going to take the chance and go after you the very first opportunity I got."

If he wasn't already hard, his dick would have been rock solid instantly. He groaned against her mouth as she leaned down and kissed him again, hard and full of passion, her hands cradling his cheeks.

"Is that OK with you?" she asked between kisses.

As way of reply, he reached up into the back of her dress and unhooked her bra, then pulled it off her body through the top of the dress, leaving her breasts covered but free for him to tease through the thin, wet fabric. With a tug he pulled the dress down and revealed taut pink nipples that he had to taste, had to lick and suck while she moaned and squirmed against him.

"I'll take that as a yes," she breathed out as he slid his hands under her dress and stroked between her legs.

"Oh yeah," he said, releasing one breast from his mouth. "That's definitely a yes." As he moved his lips to her other breast, he slid one finger into her panties, gliding through her wetness until she started to angle her hips into his finger.

The rain wouldn't last forever and eventually someone would drive by and be able to see inside the car, so rather than savor her, he knew they needed to be a little quicker than he would have preferred. He took a condom from his pocket then lifted his hips to push his clothes down enough for what was about to happen.

Slipping inside her was the sweetest sensation; she moaned as he filled her, and he savored the heat that enveloped him as he slid in. Once he was fully seated and her bottom rested against the tops of his thighs he was done for. He grabbed hold of her ass, and she grabbed hold of his shoulders.

"Lean forward a bit," he said as she began to rock on him. "I need to keep tasting you."

The motion of leaning in meant that she lifted her body then glided back down him as he continued feasting on her breasts, sucking and licking each nipple in turn.

"Is that good?" she whispered between gasping breaths. "Because... it feels... really good... to me."

Digging his fingers into her hips and her ass, he yanked her down, thrusting up into her at the same time. Her rapid breaths mingled with mewling noises and moans of pleasure as they built up to a frantic pace.

"Oh yeah," he said. "That's definitely good."

Watching the changes in her expression, from relaxed to near implosion, was just as hot as the sex itself. Her eyes drifted closed as her head lolled forward, her hips rocking, her pussy grinding into him and he had to take a deep breath to steady himself. It wouldn't serve anyone well for him to get off before she had the chance, but damn, it would take all his concentration and effort not to come inside this woman as she worked herself so close to the edge.

The rain pelted the car and thunder rolled. The lovers grunted, gasped, and groaned. Together it created the perfect soundtrack to the primal fucking that steamed up the windows by the side of an empty mountain road.

Victoria's breathing kicked up, whimpers turned to frantic grasps as she sunk her fingers into his shoulders, used him for leverage as she bounced on him, getting closer and closer to orgasm with every desperate movement.

"Oh, God," he whispered, watching her getting ready to fall over the edge.

He locked eyes with her and held her gaze as her face crumpled, her eyes slammed shut, and her head fell forward. With a scream, her entire body shuddered with the intensity of her orgasm. In direct response, Aaron thrust up into her one more time and fell into the ecstasy of his own release.

She collapsed against his chest, snuggling her nose into the crook of his neck, and stayed there while he stroked her back, helping to calm her rapid heart rate.

His own heart felt as if it would beat right out of his body. Everything about the woman on his lap turned him on and at the same time, made him feel seen for who he was. He never wanted her to know the truth, yet, if he was going to convince her to give them a try, he'd have to tell her before she figured it out on her own. But for the moment, he just wanted to hold her for as long as he could.

From her relaxed position on his chest, she said, "Thanks for that." She giggled. "I hope you didn't mind losing air hockey."

"For that?" he said and placed a kiss on the top of her head. "I will willingly throw every game of everything we ever play if that's what I get as the loser." She was soft and cozy in his arms, and he wrapped his arms tighter until she finally pushed herself back up to sitting.

"Who are you?" she asked, tilting her head and narrowing her gaze at him.

Ice water pumped through his previously fire-filled veins. "What do you mean? I already told you who I am."

Her expression was thoughtful as she worried her bottom lip between her teeth, studying his face, then reached up and trailed her fingers down his cheeks and his neck. "I know your name, but there's something you're not telling me about yourself."

"What do you want to know? I'm a guy who plays the guitar and I had a pretty decent career and now I'm enjoying being a semi-retired record producer and helping my kid chase a dream. There's not much more to tell."

His smile felt forced as he leaned away from her. There was so much more to tell but he wasn't ready for things to change between them. He wasn't ready to see the change in her eyes when she looked at him, or worse feel her body respond differently to him just because he was famous. There was no way any of those things could be the same once she knew, because how could they?

Victoria

H e didn't owe her anything. They weren't a couple, and they had no future together, so she stuffed down the frustrated sigh that simmered in her chest. After all, they'd only known each other for a week and after Sunday it wasn't like they'd ever see each other again. They were free to be whomever they had each decided to be. But it still hurt. There was something he didn't trust her to know and even after what they'd just shared, he wasn't willing to be truthful.

"OK," she said. "Good enough." She leaned down and kissed those soft, full lips, the same lips she would miss terribly once she left on Sunday. "Have you ever been to Boston?"

His warm hands rested on her hips as she pulled her dress back up, then climbed off him and settled in the seat next to him. "A few times," he answered. "Though I was never able to do much sight-seeing or anything, but it seemed like a nice enough city."

The invitation she wanted to extend died on her lips and she wasn't quite sure why. Could they be anything to each other beyond the week they shared in Hazelton? Was that what she wanted? Was that what he

wanted? Could she trust him when he obviously had a skeleton or two
in his closet? Her mind had no answers for those questions, and she
was afraid of what her heart would say, so she didn't ask it.

"It is a nice city," she said.

W hen they made it back to the Faraway, the parking lot was
mostly empty, except for her car and Aaron's daughter's.
Earlier in the day she had overheard the other guests talking about the
rehearsal dinner they were attending that night, so aside from Alyssa,
the entire inn was empty.

She had straightened her wet hair as best she could on the drive
back, having put herself back together while Aaron drove. Men had
it so much easier on that front.

He held her hand as they crossed the parking lot, being careful to
avoid the puddles that had formed during the storm, and he held the
door open for her, letting her enter the inn first. A pair of eyes met hers
immediately and Victoria knew Alyssa was keenly aware of what was
happening between herself and Aaron.

Alyssa's face broke into a huge smile, friendly and not at all angry,
the way Victoria had been anticipating. "Hey guys," Alyssa said, laying
her e-reader onto the coffee table and standing to greet them. "I was
starting to worry that maybe you got caught in the rain." She eyed
Victoria's scraggly hair and grinned. "Looks like you did."

"Hi, Lyss," Aaron said as he entered the building. "What are you
still doing up?"

Alyssa laughed. "Dad, it's only nine-thirty. I'm not quite ready to
call it a day yet." She picked up her reader from the table, tucked it

under her arm. "But, now that you're home, I think I'll head up and do a little reading before bed." She looked from one of the to the other. "Sleep well," she said and turned and walked up the stairs.

Victoria looked at him. "She knows."

"She knows what?"

"About us," she said, waving her hand back and forth between them. "She totally knows we're having sex."

His face was entirely placid. "And?"

"You don't care?" Her blood pumped furiously in her ears. She didn't have children and she'd only dated one man who had them, but she'd never even met them, so this was a new situation for her.

"No," he said. When she gave him her best shocked face, he continued. "Victoria, we're all adults here. Including my daughter. I'm pretty sure she and her partner are having sex too, because, you know... adults."

Still a bit stunned by his nonchalance, she doubled down on her decision not to spend the night in his room, nor would he spend the night in hers. She only sort of knew Aaron and she didn't know his daughter at all. The idea of them having sex with his daughter only a room or two away was a complete non-starter.

He took her hand and gently pulled her in close, wrapping his arms around her waist. "You all right?" he asked.

She nodded. "Fine. Just a little bit cold from the rain. I think I'll go up and soak in a hot bath for a while." Raising her eyes to meet his, she said, "Thank you. This was an amazing way to celebrate my birthday." As she took a step back, she placed one lingering kiss on his cheek, breathing in the rain-soaked smell of him, then said, "Good night, Aaron. I'll see you at breakfast in the morning?"

"I'll be the one with the goofy grin waiting in the dining room for you." His smile put her a little more at ease, and she knew she'd be having sweet dreams when she finally laid down for the night. "Good night, Victoria. Happy birthday."

Aaron

He couldn't say he wasn't disappointed, but he saw how uncomfortable Victoria was once she realized Alyssa knew what was happening between them. As much as he wanted to continue what they started in the car, or even hop in that hot bath with her, it was obviously not going to happen. Instead, he heaved a sigh, snagged a cookie from Hattie's table, and went into the game room to shoot a few rounds of pool, hoping to work his need for Victoria Lathrop out of his system.

An hour later he gave up trying. The harder he tried not to think about her, the clearer her image formed in his mind. The way her eyes closed as she shuddered through her orgasm, the way her whole body relaxed against him, fitted perfectly against his own. How did this random woman capture his imagination so quickly in a way nobody ever had before?

"She's really pretty."

Aaron dropped his pool cue and spun to see Alyssa leaning against the door jamb, arms crossed, a soft smile fixed to her face.

"Jeez, Lyss, don't sneak up on your old man like that. I almost had a heart attack," he said with a laugh as he retrieved the cue from the floor.

With a generous eye roll, she said, "Don't be so dramatic. You're just fine." Stepping into the room, she said, "Do you think you'll see her once she leaves here?"

He wished he had a definitive answer for her, but it wasn't something they had even talked about. He shook his head. "No idea."

"But you know where she lives, right?"

"Only that she lives and works in Boston."

"As long as you got her number, you can just text and ask her. Or you can just ask her before she leaves on Sunday."

He narrowed his eyes at her. "How do you know when she's leaving?"

"Hattie told me." She chuckled. "I think she's hoping you two will get together. She hasn't stopped giving me ideas on how to make sure that happens." Her soft chuckle turned into a laugh. "That woman has a serious match-making streak in her. She says it's part of being an innkeeper."

"I guess we'll just have to wait and see what happens."

Victoria

There was nothing quite like a hot, soaking, lavender-scented bubble bath after coming in from the cold rain. Wrapped up in her ultra-comfy robe with her hair twisted on top of her head in a towel, she needed to distract herself from thoughts of Aaron so she could finally lay down and get some sleep. Grabbing the remote, she clicked on the television from her perch on the side of the bed.

"Ugh," she said, changing the channel. "No news."

The next channel she clicked to was on a commercial, so she left it there to go brush her teeth. As she walked by the TV into the bathroom, she heard the next commercial start up.

"On this episode of *Whatever Happened To...*, we take an up-close look into the personal lives of rock music's best and most influential artists, following along through their struggles, setbacks, and successes. Tonight's profile: Undercover Angel."

"Wow, there's a blast from the past," she said to herself as she stuck her toothbrush into her mouth. She had always been more of a pop music fan as a teenager, but her younger sister was a total rock and roll girl and absolutely loved Undercover Angel. At one point Missy had an entire wall of her bedroom dedicated to pictures of the guys in the band that drove her mother crazy but made Missy happy.

Victoria smiled at the memory of her sister's obsession with a bunch of rock musicians, and she decided to watch the show to find out whatever did happen to all those rockers. It would give them something to talk about the next time they saw each other, if nothing else. The show started by profiling each member of the band as Victoria went about getting ready for bed; facial moisturizer, hand lotion, and special foot moisturizer to keep her feet sandal ready.

As she climbed into bed, the narrator moved on from the wild-man drummer to "the surprisingly quiet guitar player who truly came alive when the lights went down, Aaron Price. A California kid, Price spent his early years..." But Victoria didn't hear any of the other words as they were drowned out by the blood whooshing through her ears. The foot lotion bottle clunked to the floor as she stared at the screen, focused her eyes on the younger, longer haired version of her new lover, playing the guitar, jumping all around the stage, singing into the mic, being a rock star.

She let out a deep exhale and wondered what the hell she was supposed to do next.

Her eyes began to hurt, and she blinked a few times, suddenly aware that she hadn't done that in a while. She picked up her phone and sent off a text to Paige.

> He's a rock star.

> Is that a euphemism for something? lol

> No literally he's a rock star

???

Ever heard of Undercover Angel?

STOP IT!!!!

He was their guitar player

NO WAY!! Tell me you're not having sex with Aaron Price??!!?!?!?!?!?

That solidified it. It wasn't a dream, and she really was sleeping with the guitarist of Undercover Angel. How the hell was any of this even possible?

yes

She waited for Paige to come back with some sort of helpful advice or a funny joke or something, but there was no response. Victoria imagined she was rolling on the floor laughing at the complete mess she'd made of her love life in the name of a rebellious vacation fling.

The selfie with the guy at the bar sure made a whole lot more sense now. It also explained how a guitar player had enough extra money to buy his kid a bed and breakfast.

When her phone rang, with numb fingers, Victoria answered.

"Tell me you're joking, Vic," Paige said.

"I wish I was."

"What? Why?"

"Paige, what am I supposed to do now? I met this amazing guy on my vacation, and it turns out he's this super famous musician... Like world famous... And I had no idea. He must think I'm a complete idiot." She sighed. "Now what do I do? *'Hey, Mr. Rock Star, can I have your number? I promise I'm not a groupie and I really just like you for you, not your millions of freaking dollars.'*"

"Stop it, Vic. Does he know that you know?"

Starting at the screen and fiddling absentmindedly with the tie on her bathrobe, she shook her head, remembered Paige couldn't see her. "No. I sort of suspected there was something he wasn't telling me, but he just said he made his living playing the guitar."

"I'll say he did," Paige threw in with a laugh. "My sister and I freaking loved those guys. We saw them every time they played here."

"My sister did too."

She was suddenly exhausted and ready to cry and full of rage and she didn't know what to do with any of it. How the hell was she supposed to eat breakfast across from him in the morning?

"What do I do?" she asked again.

"Ask him to autograph your tits?"

"Paige, I'm serious!"

"I know, I know. I'm sorry," Paige said. "I guess you could pretend you didn't find out and just spend tomorrow with him as if it was any other day. Or—and hear me out on this—you could tell him you found out and ask why he didn't tell you himself. How did you find out, by the way?"

"You know the show *Whatever Happened To...*? It's on right now and it's all about Undercover Angel."

"Oh," she said. "Wait! You didn't even Google him before you went on a date with him?" Paige yelled. "What if he was a serial killer?"

Victoria laughed. "I didn't Google him. I guess I should have. But truthfully, I'm glad I didn't. The past week has been so much fun. I think that would have ruined it. Kinda like it suddenly did tonight."

"Sorry," Paige said. "Anything I can do?"

"Nah, I think I'm just going to go to bed and let my brain think on it while I'm sleeping."

"Night, Vic. Love you."

"Night, Paige. Love you too."

She held her phone in one hand and stared at it, fingers hovering above the keyboard. It wouldn't take long to bring up a million results for Aaron Price if she did search for him. Did she want to do that? Her brain was equal parts mad at him for not telling her who he was, and then grateful he didn't say anything, allowing them to get to know each other and enjoy each other over the past week. Maybe she owed it to him to learn about him from him, and not from a search engine.

After setting the phone down to charge, she clicked up the volume on the television and watched the rest of the show. Picture after picture and video after video of Aaron and the other guys in the band with a million different women couldn't be ignored. Thankfully the footage didn't show any drug use, but there was plenty of alcohol and stories of several of his band mates completely imploding and bankrupting themselves with their vices and foolish business ventures.

Sonofabitch, why did her mother have to be right about everything?

His past was nothing she had control over, but she'd be damned if she was willing to be another link in the chain of women he and his band mates had a history of using and losing. Shutting the television off, she pulled the covers over her head and tossed and turned until she finally fell into a fitful sleep.

Aaron

Despite the rain of the previous night, Saturday rolled in bright and warm, the lingering humidity sure to burn off quickly. Aaron's leg bounced of its own accord as he waited for Victoria to come down for breakfast. He'd thought a lot about Alyssa's advice from the night before and he decided he would shoot his shot and ask Victoria about continuing whatever it was that they'd started. No commitment, no pressure, just exchange numbers and see where it went.

Hattie ambled over, sat down in the empty seat across the breakfast table from him after refilling his coffee mug. "She still sleeping or did you two already call it quits?"

He sipped his coffee and smiled at the innkeeper with the penchant for meddling in his love life. "Morning, Hattie. Getting right to the point, are we?"

"To quote someone famous, I'm sure, 'Time waits for no man,' Mr. Price. Nor, I should think, does Miss Lathrop." She peered at him over her glasses, and he found himself wondering what the older woman's future would hold.

"Hattie, what are you and Mitch going to do once you sell the inn?"

She sat back, her shoulders relaxed, and a sweet smile replaced the stern look she'd been wearing. "We have a little place up by the ocean in Maine. It's not much, just a few rooms and a bath, but it's less than ten minutes away from our youngest daughter. She and her family live up there and Mitch and I are counting the days until we can be there with them."

"Do you have grandchildren?"

In response to that word, Hattie's face lit up. "We do. My youngest has three boys, my middle has two girls and my oldest has one of each. Good kids, each of them."

Quickly doing the math, he said, "Wow, seven grandkids. I can't even imagine that."

"Is Alyssa your only child?" Hattie asked, reaching to the empty table behind her for a coffee cup then filling it up for herself. She left the empty cup that would be Victoria's, and Aaron felt her absence in the gesture.

"She is."

"No grandchildren then?"

"Not yet, anyway," he said. "Who knows what the future holds, though."

Hattie's eyes lifted and she focused on something behind his head. As her lips pulled into a smile, he figured Victoria had finally shown up.

"Good morning, Miss Lathrop. Did you sleep well?" Hattie asked.

Aaron turned to greet her, his smile faltering as he did.

"I did, thank you," Victoria said in response to Hattie's question. She looked at him with red-rimmed eyes. "Morning, Aaron."

Hattie stood and pulled the chair out for Victoria to sit then flipped over and filled up the empty coffee cup. Victoria smiled her thanks but didn't speak. Aaron watched her, unsure what to say, but hoping like hell her appearance had nothing to do with him or their time together.

"Everything OK?" he asked once Hattie retreated to the kitchen. "Did you sleep all right?"

Her eyes flicked up to meet his briefly. "I'm fine."

Fuck. He didn't know what, specifically, but he knew he had done something wrong. "Anything you want to talk about? Like, maybe, why you've been crying?"

"No," she said. "It's stupid." Suddenly pushing up from her chair, she grabbed her plate and approached the buffet table for some breakfast.

Aaron watched her, studied her, suddenly aware that she must have found out who he was and wondered how she knew. Probably just a stupid Google search. But why on their last day together and not their first?

Voices from the front room filled the otherwise quiet space. The couples that were in town for their family wedding had all come down to eat breakfast and he knew the pressing conversation with Victoria would have to wait.

"Morning," everyone said to him, and he to them, as they filed into the dining room, lining up behind Victoria to get food while Hattie scurried in with a fresh pot of coffee and began filling cups.

Though her plate was piled high with home fries, bacon, and pancakes, Victoria didn't eat, so much as push around bites of food that she cut but never ingested. After a few minutes she stood. "I guess I'm not all that hungry," she said. "I'll see you later."

Aaron followed her out into the main room. "Victoria, wait," he called. "I think we probably need to talk."

Surprisingly, she stopped but she didn't turn around. "Talk about what?" she said. "About the fact that you lied to me, or the fact that whatever we started here can't happen?"

He hurried to catch up to her. "First of all, I never lied to you."

The fury on her face as she turned to face him halted his next words.

"You never lied to me?" she said, rage simmering just below the surface. "I asked you straight up who you were and rather than tell me the truth you gave me some bullshit line about being 'just a musician.'"

His own anger began to burn. "I am a musician, Victoria. I just happened to find a good deal of success with my music, but that doesn't mean I'm something other than a guy who loves to play the guitar."

She shook her head and huffed out a laugh. "You're not serious right now? I watched a television show all about you last night. They don't make shows about regular guys who like to play the guitar. I'm pretty sure at one point they referred to you as a rock and roll god, whatever the hell that means."

"It doesn't mean anything," he said. "It means exactly what I said. I play the guitar and I'm good enough at it to earn a living and see the world. That's it. Nothing more, nothing less." He needed her to understand that the rock and roll god part wasn't him. It was a label put on him by other people, and it was a label he never wanted nor enjoyed.

She regarded him the way people always did when they realized he was *that* Aaron Price, completely unsure how to talk to him like a normal person. He knew right then that whatever he had imagined for a future with Victoria would never happen. How could it?

"Listen," she said. "I'm going back to Boston tomorrow. I really want to enjoy my last day of vacation. The one thing I don't want to do is argue with you, or anyone else, about anything at all. What we had this week was fun and I'd be lying if I said it wasn't, but that's all it was. A fun vacation thing that'll make a good story when I tell it over drinks with my friends."

Oof. That one hurt like a blow to the gut; the air punched from his lungs, leaving him sucking in a deep breath to try and recover.

"Wow," he said. "That's a shitty thing to say to someone."

"Oh please," she said. "Like you don't have a million stories about all the women you've slept with? You're a fucking rock star, for god's sake. Don't pretend you're all innocent and upstanding now." She all but pushed him out of the way as she retreated up to her room, leaving him hurt, confused, angry, and guilty in her wake.

"Why didn't you tell her?"

Aaron spun around. "Jesus, Lyss. You have got to stop sneaking up on me like that."

"You're dodging my question."

His defenses shot sky high. "There was nothing to tell."

"Dad..."

"I'm not having this conversation."

How did such a promising morning turn to utter shit in such a short time?

His plan to get her number? Out the window.

His plan to see if she wanted to pursue what they'd started? Dead in the water.

And the glimpse of a happy future with the sweet and lovely Victoria Lathrop—as over as his time with Undercover Angel.

Only this time it was over before it even started.

Victoria

It was a shitty thing to say to him, and her stomach burned from the guilt gnawing at her the entire time she packed. She wasn't leaving for another twenty-four hours but she was not a last-minute packer; too much stress of forgetting things.

Why hadn't he just told her who he was? She had asked him outright and rather than come clean, he kept up with his bullshit story. At the time she'd chalked it up to them not owing anything to each other, but now that she knew the truth, it felt more like a betrayal to whatever had been developing between them. And it hurt like hell to think she was the one getting serious while he obviously wasn't interested. How could he have been if he wasn't even willing to trust her enough to admit who he was.

As she stuffed her pajamas into her dirty laundry bag, she thought back to the look of hurt on Aaron's face when she told him he was nothing more than a drinking story. It was a lie. Except for Paige, nobody would ever know what happened between her and Aaron. Aside from it not being anyone else's business, she couldn't imagine a version of the story where she looked like anything other than a starstruck fangirl jumping into bed with a rock star. Not a very flattering picture for a professional and successful businesswoman who is supposed to have better judgment than that.

She grabbed a pair of light sweatpants and a loose tee shirt and threw them on, pulled her hair into a loose ponytail. No need to look nice because there was nobody to impress on the last day of vacation. Her mind wandered back to Boston, back to the office, back to the list of client work that would need to be done when she got there. "No need to end vacation early," she said to herself as she took her book, slipped into a pair of flip flops and headed down to curl up on the couch and do a little reading.

And if Aaron happened to come by while she was there, so be it. Maybe she would even apologize for being such a bitch to him.

But he didn't show up. Not at all during the day, and neither he nor Alyssa were in the dining room when Hattie and Mitch served dinner. In fact, aside from Hattie and Mitch, Victoria was the only one in the place since everyone else was at their wedding.

"Where's Aaron?" Hattie asked. "I haven't seen him around today."

"No idea," Victoria said, swallowing down a bite of chicken parmigiana. "I haven't seen him either. Guessing he and Alyssa went out for dinner somewhere."

Hattie sat down in the chair across from her and Victoria smiled despite her dark mood.

"Something go wrong with you two?"

She laughed. "There is no us two, Hattie, so, no, nothing went wrong."

Hattie's eyes held her own. "Hmm, I'm not so sure about that. On either account." With that she stood and walked away without looking back.

Aaron

He wasn't in the wrong. Just because she asked didn't mean he had to tell her. They barely knew each other; he didn't owe her anything. At least that's what he repeated to himself ad nauseam as his car rolled through the hilly towns of western Massachusetts until he arrived at the Firehouse Recording Studio.

The large, square, red brick building used to be the home of the town's Volunteer Fire Department until it moved to a brand-new building about ten years ago, when the original building had been purchased and renovated to become one of the premier recording studios outside of New York City. He'd known about Firehouse for years but had never ventured out of the city to check it out, despite the frequent invitations from its owner, an old musician friend from the Undercover Angel days.

Bill "Crash" Williams, equally named for his propensity to total every car he ever drove, as well as his speed, skill, and ferocity on a drum kit, waited for him on the overstuffed leather couch in the sitting room that used to be the fire department's office space. "Holy shit, if it's not Aaron Price, finally come to see what the music scene is all about out here in the boondocks," Crash said as he pulled Aaron in for a handshake and then a bear hug. "How the hell have you been, man? It's good to see you."

"You know me, Crash. Retired from making music and living the good life," Aaron said. And up until he met Victoria Lathrop one week ago, it was a true statement. "Doing a little producing when time allows, but not in any places nearly as cool as this." As he stood there reconnecting with his old friend over tales of long ago and who's up to what now, he couldn't shake the empty feeling in his chest. Even as they laughed at the "remember when" stories, that hollowness refused to fill with anything except regret; regret over the choices he'd made back in the day, jumping from one woman to the next to the next; regret over the amount of time he'd missed as his daughter grew up; regret over the way things ended between him and Victoria.

He needed the Firehouse. He needed to sit with his guitar and play and sing and let music heal him the way it always did. 'Music soothes the savage beast,' as they say, and the savage beast of his broken heart needed the familiar feeling of guitar strings beneath his fingers, tunes reverberating through the air around him, hopefully filling those empty places inside him that he didn't like to think about. The need to get into the booth and play gripped his every muscle and he had to force himself to stand still and keep chatting.

"So, what finally convinced you to escape the city?" Crash said. "Needed some fresh air to breathe or space to think? Maybe a little of both?"

Leaving Victoria out of the conversation, Aaron gave his friend the rundown on Alyssa's thoughts about buying the Faraway. He told him about the land, the building, the business itself, and the kinds of things he and Alyssa had talked about.

"The rooms are great," Aaron said, and a distinct memory came to mind. Sitting on the bed, Victoria was grinning at him as he looked out the peephole after the first time they had sex, her body covered by a white terrycloth bathrobe that was open just enough to see her stunning cleavage. Why did she have to look as good as she felt? "Every guest room has its own bathroom, which is a huge selling point," he added, trying to distract himself from thoughts of her.

"You think she's going to go through with it?" Crash asked. "Tell her owning her own business is the best way to go. And if she needs help filling the rooms, tell her Uncle Crash will start sending people her way. Lots of big names come up to use this place," he said, looking around the room. "Some of them from pretty far away and they'll need somewhere nice to sleep..."

"Thanks, man," Aaron said. "She hasn't made up her mind yet, but I'll tell her when I see her tonight." His heart might have felt like it was falling to pieces, but even after years apart, a friend like Crash could always be counted on to help lift him up. "What do you say, want to give me the tour?"

A sudden giddiness overtook his old friend as he clapped his hands and rubbed them together like a little kid in a candy store. "Holy shit, dude, wait until you see this place." With a clap on Aaron's back, he led him from the sitting area into the studio space, and all other thoughts were pushed out of Aaron's mind. He marveled at the control room with a sound board that looked like it belonged at NASA, and the display of instruments, guitars, cellos, even a harp, displayed across the far end of a second sitting room. He imagined the jam sessions that could happen in a space like that and his fingers started to drum against his legs.

The soundproof booth waited for him, called to him, pulling him toward the stool, headphones, and microphone the way they always did when he needed to get out of the exterior world and into the world he truly loved. It was exactly what he needed to get out of the world of Victoria Lathrop.

For the next two hours it was just two old friends, Aaron in the booth, Crash at the controls. Everything was right, his body relaxed and his mind at ease. His fingers moved over the frets and strings like water over pebbles.

His voice was as strong and clear as it ever had been. The sense of loss over what could have been poured out of him, fueling every note, every syllable until there was nothing left. The emptiness was complete, and his body slumped under the weight of it all.

Once the last note faded away, Crash nodded from the other side of the glass, leaned forward and clicked on his mic. "Aaron, man, that was fucking unbelievable." He shook his head. "I don't think you sounded that good even back in the day. Jesus, that was... I don't even know what to call it. But thanks for letting me be the one to get it down."

From his perch on the stool, Aaron said, "I really appreciate this, Crash." His guitar rested on his knee, sweat dripped down his face. "I know it's Saturday and you probably had other things to do, but this was exactly what the fucking doctor ordered."

"It's all good, man. When Aaron Price asks to come use your studio, there's really only one answer to that, right? Besides, Hannah wanted to go antiquing or some shit like that, so I should be thanking you." Crash's laugh was cut off as he let go of the switch and his whole body shook as he cracked himself up.

Despite the train wrecks most people in their professional circle tended to make of their lives, Crash had been one of the lucky ones. He and Hannah met in college, and they'd been together ever since. As far as Aaron knew, no matter how many women threw themselves at Crash over the years, he'd never been unfaithful to Hannah. "Give me all the shit you want, man. Hannah is the love of my fucking life. I don't care what the fuck you say, I'm not doing any stupid shit that'd risk losing her," Crash had said years ago when Aaron and the rest of the guys had made fun of him for turning down a girl so hot the sidewalk melted beneath her feet. "Though it would be nice if the world would stop throwing girls like that in my face!"

The two men sat in the wooden patio chairs behind the building, a six pack between them. The heat of the late afternoon sun warmed Aaron's face as he reached for a beer. "How the hell did we ever make it through those years?" Aaron asked, tipping his bottle for a long drink.

"Beats the hell out of me," Crash said. "I fell like I could be dead five times over and somehow I'm still here."

"I think that's only because you were afraid of Hannah following you into the afterlife to kick your ass if you died doing something stupid."

Crash laughed. "Ain't that the truth of it, though?"

"Hey, Crash, I gotta ask. In all the years you've been together, was she ever weirded out by who you were?"

Crash stared at him; one brow quirked. "The fuck does that mean?"

"Nah, man, I don't mean there's anything wrong with you. I meant more, back in the day. Did she ever struggle with your fame or anything like that?"

"You'd have to ask her. I never noticed her being weird or anything. Probably it was the exact opposite, though. From where I stood, she was the one person who kept my head level. Kept me from turning into some kind of prick just 'cuz I got famous." Crash took a swig from his beer. "Why do you ask? You got trouble with a lady who's only into the rock star thing? That sucks, man."

Aaron leaned into the chair, let the sun warm his face and his arms. "I'm not sure, actually. She only just found out about me and that was kind of the end for us."

"Shit," Crash said after a few seconds. "That's not how it usually works. Don't they want to get with you once they find out who you are, not break up with you because of it?"

"Usually," Aaron said. "But not always, I guess."

"Her loss, man," Crash said, lifting his bottle for Aaron to clink his against.

"Right," Aaron said quietly. "Her loss."

Victoria

Sunday morning, Victoria stood outside Aaron's door, hand in the air, poised to knock. Her head drooped and she brought her hand down by her side, knowing full well she couldn't do it. What good would an apology be after the things she'd said to him? Especially after he made his feelings clear by being completely absent the day before.

After turning in her key and giving Hattie a quick hug, she hustled out the door before she had time to change her mind and find Aaron to say goodbye.

The return trip down the Mass Turnpike was stepping out of one world, green and alive and slow-moving, into another, gray and artificial and always moving at warp speed. She hadn't understood the difference between them before but as she got closer to home, her time at the Faraway Inn started to feel like it happened in a different lifetime. She turned up the volume, swallowed down the disappointment, and took comfort in the familiar confinement of the city.

"Welcome back!" Paige greeted her with a hug, a muffin, and a large coffee, extra sugar, when she returned to the office the day after coming home from her life-changing week away. "Tell me all about it. Tell me all about *him*."

Victoria had gotten to work early that morning to get back into the swing of things but when Paige settled into the chair across from her desk to hear the whole story, all thoughts of work were replaced by memories of her week with Aaron.

"It was amazing. He was amazing." She broke off a bite of muffin, washed it down with a sip of her coffee. "But it's over." It had to be over, and she needed to let it be.

"What do you mean it's over? Did you not sleep with Aaron Price last week?"

"Yes."

"More than once?"

"...Yes..."

"And...?"

"And nothing. There is no and. We met, we had sex, he lied to me, I came home. Easy as that."

Paige adjusted her position in the chair, settling in for a longer story than Victoria was ready to tell. It had only been a few days and she still hadn't gotten through the ever-present dark cloud of frustration about how things turned out.

"He lied to you. Lied about what?" Paige asked. Her eyes softened and a small smile pulled at her lips. "Oh, God. Did he tell you he loved you even though it was only like two dates?" She shook her head, understanding written all over her face. "He was one of those super needy guys?"

Victoria laughed. "No, he didn't tell me he loved me. And he wasn't needy at all. He was a really nice guy. I liked him. A lot."

"Wow," Paige said. "That's something you've never said before. At least not as long as I've known you. So, what went wrong?"

"There was something about him, you know? Like he was obviously good looking, but he just sort of had this way about him. I can't quite name it. But then one night we were out at this restaurant, a local brewery that was so cool, you would love it. Anyway, on his way back from the men's room he stopped to talk to a few people. It was like they knew him." She felt the shame of her stupidity. "Later that night I asked him outright who he was, and he told me he was just a musician."

Paige interrupted her. "I would like to point out again that Google exists, Vic. Why didn't you just look him up?"

"I don't know," she admitted. "Like I said the other night, I guess I wanted him to tell me. I didn't want to snoop around behind his back." It felt invasive to go behind his back and see what the world said he was before he had a chance to show her for himself.

"Umm, ten bucks says he looked you up within an hour of meeting you."

What a terrible thought. "I hope not," she said. "Why would he do that?"

"Like most people, he probably wanted to make sure you weren't some kind of serial killer." Paige was smiling and Victoria wasn't sure if she was kidding or not.

Somehow the thought of Aaron looking her up online and pre-judging her made her even sadder than she was before.

"You listen to too many true crime podcasts," Victoria said, then leaned back in her big black leather chair. "Moving on... what's on the docket for today? Being in the mountains for a week feels like I'm coming back after a year on the moon."

The women laughed together, and Paige filled her in on everything she'd missed while she was off "getting freaky with a rock star." Which clients had issues, which had requests, and what still needed to be done for a couple of potential clients.

Over the course of an hour, the office filled up as employees showed up, keyboards clacked, and conversations brought life to the space. "Morning, Vic," people would call out on the way to their workstations. "How was vacation?"

The familiarity of the noises was comforting, normal. The groove of work and even the pain-in-the-ass clients that needed a little extra hand holding all felt good. It all felt right. It was where she belonged and maybe it was for the best that things with Aaron hadn't worked out. Maybe not working out was the best thing for her, for both of them.

Aaron

"It's been a real pleasure having you stay here with us, Mr. Price," Hattie said as she handed him his paperwork and took back his room key. He still had two days left of his vacation but being in the Faraway without Victoria wasn't fun anymore.

"Thanks, Hattie. You and Mitch have been more than accommodating. I appreciate you letting me and Alyssa peek behind the curtain."

"Oh, it was our pleasure. But I do have to ask if you think she's interested." She was quick to add in, "No pressure at all. Just, if she's not, we'll probably get to work getting the place listed by the end of August."

"She has a meeting set up with an accountant on Monday, then we have another meeting set up with her bank to talk finances on Wednesday. Would you mind giving her until Friday to take it all in and make a decision?"

"Friday's perfect," Hattie said.

Everywhere he looked inside the inn brought memories of Victoria. They'd only known each other for a week, yet everything was a reminder of her. The stairs where they met, the game room where he played her for the privilege of buying her dinner. A smile tugged at his lips as he walked onto the front porch, and what he now considered Victoria's swing, sat vacant while the memory of her birthday morning played like a movie on the screen of his mind. The way her eyes fixed on him while he sang to her, the sparkle in her eye when she made her wish.

Every step across the driveway was a step further away from his time with Victoria. Each was a step closer to his old life, his life before he knew her. One week. It was one fucking week. He'd had longer relationships than that and not felt any feelings one way or another when they ended. Why was Victoria Lathrop so hard to let go of. Clearly, she was all right with letting him go, so, why couldn't he return the gesture? And why did her comment about him being nothing more than a drinking story piss him off as much as it did? She wasn't wrong about the countless women he'd been with over the years, but even so, it felt like a knife in his heart when she thought she meant nothing more than that to him.

Crash had done a bit of clean up work to the tracks he laid down and Aaron cued them up to play as he pulled out of the parking lot and headed toward the highway. A rush of memories and feelings came flooding back as the power and emotion in his own voice washed over him. Being without Victoria felt like being without music. It certainly wasn't a way he wanted to live but she'd made her feelings clear on the subject and he'd have to figure out how to forget her and move on with his life.

Once he was back home and settled into his old routine for a few days, his pressing need for Victoria began to fade into the background. Rather than the constant crashing of cymbals, it was more a steady, quiet bass line that underpinned everything he did. From cooking and washing dishes, to doing laundry and making his bed, the constant strum of longing was his company.

"I'm still not sure," Alyssa said as they walked out of the bank on Wednesday afternoon. "I mean, I know I can do the work," she said tentatively. "But what happens if I get sick or Ben and I get married and I need to go on a honeymoon or what if I just need a day off?" She shook her head, thinking of all the possibilities. "But then, what if I say no to this and I regret it forever and ever?"

Aaron had known she and Ben were still together but he hadn't known they'd talked marriage. "So, if you decide to do this, would Ben be going to Hazelton with you?"

Her face broke into a huge smile. "He would. He's lucky enough to be able to work from anywhere so he would totally come with me." The smile faltered. "But he's been totally up front with me saying he wasn't interested in being an innkeeper. He'll help me do the small stuff, but the landscaping and all that kind of big stuff? I'll have to hire people for that."

"Which is another expense?" Aaron guessed.

"Yup."

He put an arm around her shoulders and hugged her, letting her rest her head against his chest. She wasn't a child anymore but he couldn't resist the urge to kiss the top of her head. "Whatever you decide will be the right choice." He squeezed her shoulders. "I have all the faith in the world that you can do this. And if you choose not to, whatever you do next will be amazing."

"Thanks, Dad." He walked her to her car. Before she drove away, she opened her window and said, "Hey, have you heard from Victoria since you got home?"

The downtown area was full of people, walking and driving all around, yet all at once the only sound he heard was his heartbeat in his own ears.

· ♥ · ♥ · ♥ · ♥ · ♥ ·

H is sprawling back yard lay before him as he sat outside with his guitar and a tall glass of lemonade. The low sun had almost entirely sunk behind the mountains in the distance when Aaron's phone pinged a text notification.

Hey Dad I made a decision.

Victoria

Weeks came and went, the rhythm and routine of her work kept Victoria busy and preoccupied during the day, but still the nights were more difficult. She thought Aaron would have worked himself out of her system by the time September rolled around. So, why hadn't he? Why did she still miss that stunning smile, those strong hands, the broad shoulders? Why did she miss the way he felt when he held her? Why did she miss the way *she* felt when he held her?

Thinking she was just feeling lonely, she agreed to a date with a man who'd found her online dating profile. Her complete lack of enthusiasm as she dressed and did her makeup should have been her first clue to cancel the date, but there was no way to know if simple loneliness was causing her to hold onto her fledgling feelings for Aaron.

Jack was a nice enough man, polite and kind. He had good manners and didn't pressure her for a kiss, or anything else, when the date ended. He also didn't ask when they could see each other again. Rather than be disappointed, she was relieved. At least now she knew. It wasn't loneliness. He just wasn't Aaron.

After a quick shower, she sat in her robe, her laptop open, a glass of pinot beside her for a little extra courage, and typed his name into the search bar. She wasn't looking for dirt on him or bad stories to convince herself she was better off without him. She simply needed to see him, to look at that face again.

Most of the results were focused on Aaron and his time with Undercover Angel so she searched again to find entries about him alone. Several were click-bait type headlines which her fingers hovered over for a split second, but she scrolled past until a link to a video won the day.

As she watched the footage of Aaron playing some little club, just him and his guitar, her heart broke all over again. The difference between Aaron the rock star that had been profiled on television and Aaron the musician was striking. When he was playing with the band, he was great, full of energy and fun; a stereotypical rock star. But when it was just him, sitting on a stool in front of a small crowd, he was amazing. He was still having fun but his whole countenance was different, he was comfortable, alive, and at peace up there. Exactly the way he looked when he played for her on her birthday.

A beautiful smile and relaxed posture told Victoria everything she needed to know about him. Whoever took the video of him had a fairly steady hand and when Aaron looked directly into the camera, he looked directly at Victoria, her eyes suddenly watery, and she kicked herself for not getting his number before she left Hazelton.

There was no way she could ever get it now. Someone as famous as that surely was not listed anywhere she could find it.

Her only hope was Hattie.

"Sorry, Miss Lathrop. That's not something I can give you." Hattie sighed and Victoria heard the sadness and frustration in the older woman's voice. "I really wish I could."

"Right. I understand." And she did. "Thanks anyway."

With that, Victoria filed away Aaron Price as an exciting adventure in a well-lived life and went back to living.

"Alright, Paige, I'm taking off. See you Tuesday." Having enjoyed her creativity-focused solo vacation in the Berkshires as much as she did over the summer, Victoria decided to make it a more regular part of her calendar. There was a long weekend ahead of her and there was a reservation at a hotel by the ocean in Kennebunkport, Maine with her name on it. There was also a tour scheduled to see the ceramics collection at one of the local art galleries. Drawing hadn't come back to her the way she would have liked, so with every weekend away she tried her hand at something new.

Her bags were packed and waiting in her car. She needed only to get out of the office without any other interruptions.

"Oh, wait!" Paige called after her as she passed by her friend's desk. "You can't go yet. You have one more appointment this afternoon. Potential client, they scheduled a couple days ago."

There went her plans of starting vacation early.

"Seriously? I didn't see it on my calendar." She let her purse slip off her shoulder as she turned around to stomp back into her office like a petulant child. "Sometimes working for yourself kind of sucks," she grumbled as she slumped down into her chair to wait for the potential client to arrive. Her heart and her mind were already traveling up

Interstate 95 toward a salty ocean breeze, but her backside was firmly planted in her office chair as she needed clients like this for her own livelihood, as well as the employees who depended on her. Maine wasn't going anywhere, even if the added traffic would make her later than she would have liked.

Paige appeared in Victoria's doorway. "Right this way," Paige said, pointing into the office.

Victoria's heart stopped beating as, from just outside her doorway, a familiar, sweet-as-honey voice said, "Thank you."

It was him and yet there was no way it was him. But it sounded exactly like him. Why the hell would he be standing in her office on a random Friday afternoon? Why didn't he walk faster so she could see, once and for all, who had a voice exactly like Aaron Price but who couldn't possibly be Aaron Price?

Her entire body was suddenly filled with concrete, unable to move anything except her eyes. Aaron Price, even more handsome than she remembered him, walked in then stood in front of her desk, staring down at her wearing a most unreadable expression. In his hands he held a cardboard box with an assortment of green leaves sticking out the top.

"Victoria," he said as he placed the box of herbs onto her desk then shoved his hands into his pockets.

"Wh- what are you doing here?" she finally managed to say. Her pulse kicked up and if she wasn't lost in the shock of seeing him, she would have jumped up and thrown her arms around him. Then there was that niggling part of her brain that told her he wouldn't welcome it if she did.

His mouth pulled into a slight grin. "It's nice to see you too. How've you been?"

She stared at him, still trying to wrap her head around the fact that Aaron was in her office with a box full of plants. From behind him, Paige caught her eye, mouthed "Oh, my God," while she jokingly fanned herself then closed the door in her wake, leaving Victoria alone in the room with the man she had all but given up on.

Aaron

If the look on Victoria's face meant anything, it meant she was caught completely by surprise when he walked in the door holding a cardboard tray with a bunch of basil, oregano, and rosemary plants in terracotta pots. And judging by the purse sitting on top of her desk, keys beside it, she had been trying to leave the office when his unexpected appearance forced her to stay.

He'd almost forgotten how beautiful she was. Even though she was in her element, boss of her world, dressed to impress, she was still the same Victoria he'd come to care for all those weeks ago. Would he call it love? Could he call it love? Perhaps. But perhaps they needed a little more time together to see if that's where this ride would eventually take them.

"Am I keeping you from leaving early?" he asked, eyeing her purse and keys. "I can come back another time if this isn't convenient for you."

She still hadn't really said anything to him, and his heart ached thinking he'd made a mistake by showing up. As hard as he'd tried to keep it at bay, the thought that she meant what she said about him being a fun story to tell at parties elbowed its way back into his consciousness.

She yanked her purse off the desk and tossed it to the floor by her feet. "No," she said. "I'm not going anywhere. Well, I am going to Maine, but I don't need to leave early."

Oh, shit. She'd found someone else, someone who was currently waiting for her in Maine. The silence between them stretched on impossibly long and he began to think he'd made a terrible mistake.

"Are those for me?" she finally said, pointing her chin at the box of herbs.

Pushing the box gently toward her, he nodded.

"Thank you." Looking around her sparsely decorated office, she said, "I still haven't gotten around to getting any of my own." Her voice didn't hint at what she was feeling as he stood in silence contemplating the best way to make a graceful exit. Or to finally put it all out on the line, tell her how he felt, and let the chips fall as they may.

"I'm really glad you're here," she said.

"You are?"

Finally, a smile made its way across her face, her eyes lighting up the way he'd hoped they would as he'd driven from the Berkshires out to Boston. Finally confident that he'd made the right call in coming to see her, he slid into the chair in front of her desk.

"I can't stop thinking about you," she said in a soft voice. "I wonder what you're doing all the time." She dropped her head, studied the floor in front of her. "I wonder if you're thinking about us... about me."

When she raised her gaze to meet his again, any doubts he'd had about them as a couple went out the window. There was no doubt whatsoever that she was worth any risk. She was worth putting his heart on the line for. She was the one woman he wanted more than anything else.

"I haven't stopped thinking about you since you left the Faraway," he said. "And I haven't stopped hating myself for not being man enough to try and stop you that day."

She shook her head, her brows furrowed. "Aaron, I said some horrible things to you, and I am so sorry for that. I never expected you to try and stop me. In fact, I've been beating myself up for not having the courage to apologize to you before I left. I..." She paused. "I tried calling Hattie the other day to get your number. I knew she couldn't give it to me, but I also kind of hoped that if she saw you again, she might tell you I was looking for you."

It was time to start being completely honest with her. "She didn't have to tell me. I was standing right next to her when you called."

Victoria's face pulled into a frown. "Why were you at the Faraway? And wait, why didn't you let her give me your number?"

He loved the fire that burned in her eyes at that moment. He loved the way she got right to the point. The intensity on her face sparked an instant fire in his gut. He wanted her more at that very moment than he'd wanted her during their entire week together at the Faraway, and he had wanted her bad enough then that he could taste it.

"I wish your office was empty right now," he said.

Her frown transformed to a look of confusion as her brows knit together. "What? Why?"

He leaned forward and ran his hands over the smooth desktop. "Because I really want to bend you over this desk and take you right here. I wouldn't even take off your clothes... just lift your skirt and slide your panties to the side." He was hard instantly thinking about her bent over, feet apart, hands splayed as he drove into her.

She swallowed audibly and he knew she wanted it just as much as he did. He also knew she was a professional and it would never happen while her employees were working on the other side of the door. As if to prove his theory, a chorus of laughter rose up from the people working in the main office and Victoria's face changed. She shook off her lust and, with a deep breath, returned to her professional self.

"As much as I would enjoy that, maybe this isn't quite the time or place for bending me over and sliding my panties to the side."

He chuckled. "I think you're right about not being the time, but this is one hundred percent the right place." He eyed the desk. "Height looks right. And you would look perfect leaning over it with your ass in the air," he said, nodding. "No, this is definitely the right place."

She wriggled in her seat, and he knew she was entertaining the idea, so he decided to keep her in that heightened state of need that couldn't come close to matching his own. "Anyway," he said. "About my reason for being here." Reaching into his pocket, he pulled out his phone and scrolled until he found what he was looking for. "I find myself in need of a social media manager for a small business I've recently invested in, and your firm comes highly recommended." He spun the phone and slid it across the desk for her to see.

Victoria

The smiling face of his daughter standing in front of the Faraway Inn sign with a big, red SOLD placard across the top stared back at her.

"No way! You actually did it." She jumped up from behind her desk and hopped into his lap, throwing her arms around his neck, as natural as if they'd done it every day. Snuggling her nose into the crook of his neck, she stole a quick sniff, taking in his distinct scent, lighting a streak of fire directly down her middle. "That's fantastic. Alyssa must be so excited to have all those lonely hearts to fix come Christmas time."

His laughter warmed her and when she tried to release her hug, she found herself tugged down and held firmly in his lap. "I like you better here," he said into the back of her neck. "I think maybe we should have our whole business meeting like this."

Oh, how she wanted to tell him she was all in. She wanted to turn toward him, hold his beautiful face, and kiss him until he couldn't see straight.

But she couldn't do that. Not yet. There were still a few things she needed to know.

"That would be nice, but…"

He kissed the back of her neck, took a nibbling taste of that spot where her neck met her shoulder. "But you need to know why I didn't tell you who I was."

"Who you are," she corrected.

"Right," he said. "Who I am."

"And why you wouldn't let Hattie give me your number. That's the other big thing, especially if you were standing right next to her. You need to tell me what that was all about, Mr. Rock Star."

His little laugh blew a breath through her hair, which fanned that spark through the rest of her. Then when he squeezed her a little tighter, she snuggled into his body and waited for him to talk.

"You were right," he said. "When you came right out and asked, I should have told you. I'm not sure why I didn't. And I'm sorry for that. I was thrown off guard with you and I was having so much fun. And I think, after a lifetime of experience being me, I guess, in part, I figured you must've already known. I mean, who doesn't Google a person before they go on a date with them?"

"Me," she said in a quiet voice.

"Well, you should." He squeezed his arms around her middle and kissed the spot behind her ear.

She leaned back against his chest. "Because you never know how many dates I could have with guys that are secretly rock stars looking for love?"

He grunted. "Stop calling me that." After kissing her cheek, he added, "And, no, you should Google them to make sure they're not some kind of criminal or something. Victoria, you work in tech for a living. How do you not know this stuff?"

She sighed. "I do know this stuff. I guess I just wanted you to tell me. I didn't want to have to base my opinion of you on whatever search results turned up. I wanted to get to know you for you."

"And that's also why I didn't say anything. Because you didn't know me. You had no expectations of what it would be like to be with me, and you let yourself know me for who I am now, not who I used to be ten years ago. Obviously, I'm still the same person, and I take full responsibility for all the decisions I've made, both good and bad. But a lot of that persona was exactly that, a persona. It was just for show. It was how I needed to act to make it look like I was loving life. But this me? The man you know? This is who I am now."

Stroking his finger over her arm, he said, "I'm just a guy who happens to be falling for the incredibly sexy and talented and smart and stunningly beautiful entrepreneur sitting in his lap."

The deep rich tone of his voice was like honey as she took in his words. Falling for her? Her heart kicked up as she realized they were falling for each other. Together. "Thank you," she said. "And the part about Hattie?"

"Oh that? That's an easy one. I didn't want you to call me because I wanted to drive out here to see you. I wanted to catch you off guard so I could watch you react when I walked in the door. You're very easy to read."

His fingers trailed lightly up her arms and anticipatory sparks raced through her body as she snuggled back against him, loving the soft caress that hinted at so much more. "You know," she said, "I have a room rented up by the ocean for the weekend. If we leave now, we can get there before dinner."

"Meaning?"

"Meaning there will be plenty of time to discuss your business needs as we drive and then plenty of time to get naked before we even have time to get hungry," she said.

His strong, warm hands cupped her breasts, slid down and began to caress her inner thighs. "What if I told you I'm hungry now?" he asked as he tasted the sensitive skin behind her ear.

Every ounce of control she'd worked so hard to maintain faded into nothingness with her body pressed against his. When his fingers made their way into her panties, she said, "I'd say if you go lock the door, I'll pull the window shades."

"**D**o you have more condoms?" she asked as they drove up toward Maine in the afterglow of silent, secretive sex. Her body still burned from the sheer eroticism of what transpired in her office. "Because I think we're going to need a whole lot more."

Victoria

One Year Later

Another summer had come to a close, and with it came the biggest change of the past year. Earlier that morning the general contractor had handed over the keys to Victoria and Aaron's new cottage, tucked into a far corner of the Faraway Inn's three-acre property.

The past year with Aaron had been a whirlwind of changes and excitement, learning about each other as they navigated their new and unexpected love. Introducing him to her family had been more fun than she'd anticipated. Her mother had loved Aaron within minutes of meeting him, and Missy had giggled like a teenager the entire time they were eating dinner.

Working in Boston three days a week, then working remotely from the Faraway the rest of the time had allowed her to be near Aaron as he helped Alyssa get set up as the new owner of the inn, as well as keep an eye on construction of their new cottage while still maintaining her clients' needs.

"You ready?" Aaron stood behind her, arms wrapped around her middle.

She had never been more ready for anything in her life.

Excitement and nervousness in equal measure flooded her body, but as Aaron spoke, his warm voice soothed her the way it always did, and she leaned back into the strength of his body and nodded.

She turned the key in the lock, and had pushed the door open, when he scooped her up in his arms, princess-style.

With a giggle, she said, "What are you doing?"

"I thought it was fairly obvious that I was about to carry the love of my life over the threshold, but if you'd rather I toss you over my shoulder and carry you like a caveman, I could do that." He shifted her in his arms, as if was about to do just that.

She grabbed onto his neck and held on. "No," she said with a laugh. "This is fine."

"Good." With her in his arms, he stepped into the cottage, turned, and used her dangling feet to push the door closed behind them.

She'd been inside countless times over the months of its construction but now that it was theirs officially, it felt different. Even without any of their furniture or belongings it felt like home. The hardwood floors reflected the sun as it blazed through the giant windows and Victoria could imagine where everything would go when it was finally delivered over the coming weeks.

But there was still something that wasn't clicking.

Then she suddenly understood. "I think it's you," she said as he set her down in the middle of the empty living room.

"What's me?"

"Well, I was just thinking how much this place feels like home but it's only an empty house, so how could that be? And then I realized it's not the house that feels like home, it's you. You feel like home."

Reaching up to her tiptoes to place a kiss on his cheek, she said, "Do you remember last year on my birthday you brought me the muffin Hattie made and I wished on it?"

"Of course."

"This is what I wished for... in a roundabout way." She knew that wouldn't make sense to him, so she explained further. "Before you came out to sing to me that morning, I was journaling and thinking a lot about a missing piece." She placed a hand on her chest above her heart. "I didn't know what was causing that feeling and I didn't know how to deal with it. So, I made my wish that the universe would tell me what I was missing. Only it did me one better and gave me you."

He leaned down and kissed her so gently it felt like a butterfly had landed on her lips. "I love you, Victoria, so so much. Thank you for taking a chance on an old rock star like me."

"This might actually be the best day of my life," she whispered against his chest. "I love you so much."

She could have stayed in his arms for the rest of the day, but he had other plans. "It's not over yet," he said into the top of her head. "I do have a surprise for you in the studio."

Victoria squeezed him a little tighter and murmured into his chest, "I like the sound of that."

Chuckling, he said, "I knew you would, but it's not that kind of a surprise."

Leaning back so she could look up into his eyes, she quirked her eyebrow, waited for him to explain.

"Come on," he said, taking her by the hand, and led her toward the back of the cottage. Across a small, paved walkway was a soundproof music studio that Aaron had added to the plans so he could make, record, and produce music without leaving home. "It's in here." He pushed the door open, and they entered the empty space that would eventually be a casual living room at the front of the building. Off to the side, against one wall stood a brand-new, full-size air hockey table. Framed on the wall above it was a hand drawn rosemary plant on notebook paper.

"You didn't." Her heart melted as his thoughtfulness showed through once again in the things he did for her. "This is amazing!" She threw her arms around his neck and jumped into his arms, covering his face in kisses. "I love it so much."

"It flips over to a pool table," he said, grinning down at her. "I figure that way we can both win now and then."

"It's perfect," she said as he set her feet back onto the floor. "Want to play right now?"

"Damn straight, I do."

Victoria went to the far end of the table and searched for the switch to turn it on. When she stood back up, Aaron was at the other end waiting for her to drop the puck. The first goal took her less than fifteen seconds, but he quickly recovered and scored on her ten seconds later.

"You've been practicing," she teased as she reached down into the cubby hole where the puck was returned, and right next to the thin plastic disc, her fingers felt and then wrapped around a small box.

"Aaron?" she said. With trembling fingers, she pulled the box out and held it in her hand. Aaron closed the distance between them in two strides.

He took the box from her outstretched palm. "Victoria, you are the most incredible person I've ever known. Your heart, your mind, your soul, your seriousness, your playfulness—all of you. I can't imagine letting another day go by without you by my side as my friend, my lover, and, I hope, my wife." He removed the ring from the box, lowered down to one knee. "Will you do me the honor of letting me be Mr. Victoria?"

Her heart felt full to bursting as she thought about how much fun it would be getting married to Aaron, how much fun it would be being married to him. "Yes," she said, nodding, wiping tears from her eyes. "A hundred times yes. A million times yes. Forever and always yes."

He slid the ring, a deep red ruby in the center of a gold band with diamonds set all around it, onto her finger then stood before her. "Thank you," he said, wrapping his arms around her again. "Thank you for making me the happiest man on the planet right now."

She stood on tiptoe and whispered into his ear, "I can make you happier..."

His grin told her he understood exactly what she meant.

Flicking a glance toward the music studio, he said "It's sound-proof."

Without another word she took his hand and together they celebrated the ending of one chapter and the beginning of the best one so far.

I hope you enjoyed Victoria and Aaron's story. If you did, please consider leaving a review at any or all of the usual places. For indie authors, reviews are our bread and butter!

And, if you sign up for my twice-monthly newsletter, Whispers and Works in Progress, you have access to all of my bonus content, including a sweet story about Aaron's over-the-top birthday celebration for his new wife.

Scan the QR code below to sign up for free today!

BOOKS BY E.A. BRADY

Berkshire Romance Series

One Week at the Faraway Inn
Picture Me Yours
Christmas at Whispering Hills

Built to Last Series

Stitches and Sparks
Barstools and Beginnings
Coffee and Kisses

Stand Alone Books

Keep Me Warm: A Christmas Novella
Print Readers – links can be found at home.eabradyauthor.com

Afterword

Growing up I was exposed to rock and roll music from a very young age. My (way cool) older brother even took me to my first rock concert as a birthday gift!

As a teenager, my bedroom walls were covered with posters of my favorite musicians—*looking at you, Jon Bon Jovi*—with a few actors thrown in for good measure.

Fast forward to being a full-on adult with young adult children, and the idea of what rock stars do with themselves when they stop being rock stars started kicking around my brain. Then I wondered what someone my own age would do if she ran into a rock star... but didn't know it.

Naturally, I decided to write a light-hearted romance about a former rock star and the type A businesswoman he meets when they are both on vacation.

The original draft of this story was written while I was stuck at home with COVID in the summer of 2022. I didn't feel 'sick' but I couldn't leave the house, so I dragged my laptop onto the back deck, threw on my favorite hairband playlists, and let my imagination free.

About the Author

Despite spending my first few years in New York, I consider myself
a New Englander, through and through. My stories are set in fiction-

alized versions of several of my favorite New England locations and my characters are "real" people who are trying their hardest to make it through to their very own happily ever after.

When I'm not working on new stories, I spend my time working on my Muay Thai round kicks and trying to perfect my left hook. I live in a 130-year-old (haunted?) house with my husband, two amazing kids, and two spoiled tabby cats. I wouldn't have it any other way.